THE HURRICANE DRIFT

Jonathan Blake was an adventurer on holiday and when the hurricane came he flew from it, taking a woman called Jo with him. But the hurricane, and the wrath of the lady's husband, follows them . . . Landing on a secret island proves to be a dangerous move, leaving Blake wondering whether to fight 'em or join 'em. When he does both, it seems that calamity is inevitable. But perhaps there is a way of escape after all . . .

JOHN NEWTON CHANCE

THE HURRICANE DRIFT

Complete and Unabridged

LINFORD
Leicester

First published in Great Britain by
Robert Hale Limited
London

First Linford Edition
published 2006
by arrangement with
Robert Hale Limited
London

British Library CIP Data

Chance, John Newton
The hurricane drift.—Large print ed.—
Linford mystery library
1. Triangles (Interpersonal relations)—
Fiction 2. Hurricanes—Fiction
3. Detective and mystery stories
4. Large type books
I. Title
823.9'14 [F]

ISBN 1–84617–524–0

Published by
F. A. Thorpe (Publishing)
Anstey, Leicestershire

Set by Words & Graphics Ltd.
Anstey, Leicestershire
Printed and bound in Great Britain by
T. J. International Ltd., Padstow, Cornwall

This book is printed on acid-free paper

1

I'm not naturally a cynic, but the romance of faraway places is to me like a pantomine, which, as a child, you have to believe in. Whenever I go anywhere, there are just people. If I go anywhere nearish, it's just English people. Anywhere farish, it's just other sorts of people. Only they all dress the same, talk about the same things and chase after the same Jones.

I think perhaps Jones is the trouble, because no one has ever found out who he is.

I did not go to the West Indies to find Jones or parallel him, but because I was tired of winter, wanted the warm rich air off the heated oceans and a feeling of wealth, which I had not got.

There was plenty of rich, warm air. After the first week on the island with the millionaires, the air started to swing.

It swung faster, began to spin. Began to wander up and down and round about the Gulf, and finally worked itself into a sizable imitation of a hurricane name of Gertie.

Most of the portable part of the island was blown into the sea and we had floods, near earthquakes and days and days of this fearful, burning, screaming, terrifying wind. It kept going and then coming back.

Every time things tried to straighten up, back came Gertie again. We mucked in, rescue work and that, and when she finally went away, I noticed that all the English had stopped talking about the terrible weather at home. I was by then keen to have some of the old familiar stuff. You may not know just when you'll get wet in Manchester, but you know roughly where you stand in relation to what comes next. It doesn't suddenly come up behind and blow your house down and your head off and leave you with your only means of escape, your car, upside down in the pineapple beds.

At the time Gertie eased away, I was on the point of cabling my bank for an advance to get me home. Perhaps originally I had had some idea of never going back, or what. I don't really remember. I had come out for the rich, warm air, impetuous like, and having had it sooner than expected, wanted to go back.

Do not think my situation is normally parlous; I have a small professional practice at home, freelance, which is good for a steady income. The only thing about that is I'm not steady myself. For my holiday I had made arrangements to have enough for all purposes except playing poker in a bomb shelter in a hurricane with four millionaires. They skinned me.

It was while downing a drink in a wrecked hotel bar that the cable arrived. It said to get in touch with Barr and Solstice, solicitors, Lincoln's Inn, urgently.

The only reason I could think of for my lawyers wanting to see me was on account of one or two past adventures which had naught to do with professional matters at all. The whole atmosphere of that broken-down, blown-out palace of illusion persuaded me of the worst.

Yet, still, I had seen too many films beginning in the lush colours of the Gulf of Mexico, where the main character inherits a fortune, mainly, I have discerned, to keep the rich background going. (If any Gerties arrive during the filming, I notice, they are ruthlessly cut out.)

I thought of my late playfellows, Harz, Gordon, Mancini and Gorse, the fellows with all the cards. Shrewd millionaires all, except in the ease with which they could be persuaded that a delicacy was something that cost a lot. They ate things the locals had been feeding the cats with for centuries and paid handsomely. They drank things that could have been, and tasted like, cocktails of throwout rum and hair oil and so long as it costs and they knew Jones the Rich drank it, it was good to them.

Sometimes I felt sorry for them. I remember once in Nagasaki — on one of my bouts of restlessness — my friend and I were served with some kind of cooked crab that turned out to be still alive. I'm not so easily bullied and walked out. He

4

stayed, ate them and was sick and couldn't sleep for weeks because he kept dreaming of things starting to walk about in his belly.

As I sat there, staring out through the range of windows to the littered beach, blinding yellow in the sun, I thought that if I had money I'd put it, not in food, but in stomach powders containing the new instant faith giver and wind dispenser.

If I had money.

So I looked at the cable, and I looked at Joey, who had left his wife in Kingston so he could beam behind the millionaire's bar. He was grinning at some dream as he gazed at the blue sea, and I guess he was thinking of his faraway wife blown out by Gertie.

Money. Could it mean money?

'Joey, another beer,' I said. 'And not one with the frozen-out flavour. Fifty-six degrees, as I told you.'

'You sure right, Mass Blake,' he said in some accent I have never been able to get set. Sometimes he could come from New Orleans, at others from a back street in Ealing, London, but rarely did he sound like coming from Kingston. 'I got myself liking it that way, sure. It don't make your teeth ache.'

As he came and put the glass on my table I saw his gold chain slave bangle slip down over his hand. Gold.

Could it be money?

What the hell else could it be?

As I sat, my arms on the chair arms, a slim and beautiful hand came to rest on mine.

'Let's go from here, rogue.'

I looked up past the beautiful bust of Jo Mancini to her brown laughing face. Her tan made her gold hair shine more like a tinted silver. She had green eyes, and there was a flash in thcm, not of silver humour, but of something much harder. She is one of the most beautiful women I have ever known and the only one I ever made love to with a hurricane actually tearing the shutters off the bedroom walls. Afterwards she said it made her day, or night, and she would gladly hire a hurricane for every time coming after.

'Drink first,' I said, getting up. 'There's

nobody here. What's the matter with here?'

So she had some mess of lime and gin and lemonade and lemon and mint and sugar and orange slices and ice which went on my bill at thirty bob plus the tip for Joey's time in thinking it all up.

But it was rich, buying drinks at thirty bob a slug and sounded even richer in dollars. Again I wondered about the cable, yet hesitated still in case it heralded some determined effort to get me back and hanged.

'Well, ask me what's the matter,' she said, her eyes gleaming over the fringe of herbage in her drink. 'Or haven't you noticed my acid?'

'I noticed everything,' I said, patting her hand on the arm of her chair. 'I feel everything you feel. I hear another Gertie is expected this afternoon.'

She smiled, but it was rather cold and calculating now.

'It's about that,' she said, looking round slowly and very gracefully. I loved the way her head sat on her long neck, and the way her neck went down —

'About Gertie?' I said, glancing at the bar. But Joey was busy and humming to himself.

She had one of those large handbags the women cart around the heat beaches of the play world, and she opened it. There was a gun inside. I looked at it with a twinge of guilt.

'I thought I lost that in rescue work,' I said.

'You left it in my room,' she said. 'And Pat found it. I said I borrowed it, but he knows.'

'Bad for Pat,' I said.

'Bad for Jonathan Blake, also,' she said calmly. 'He says he will blow your bloody head off.' She smiled. 'Perhaps I wouldn't mind that so much, but he says he's going to blow mine off, too. In fact, he's waiting to find us both together so as to save on shots.'

'Does he mean it?' I watched Joey turn his back to put something on a shelf, then I slipped the gun out of her bag and into my pocket.

'He means it,' she said, almost gaily. 'But he has to get tanked up first. You know at Harrow you're taught not to shoot your wife and her lover in cold blood.'

'He was never at Harrow,' I said. 'It's a lie. Part of the act. Why should he worry, anyway? He prefers poker to you.'

'Anything for a laugh,' she said, and finished her drink. 'But the fact is, he'll do it. Not personally, you understand.'

'You mean he'd hire a killer?' I didn't believe it, but I could feel a cold cramp round my head at the idea. When you have the Mancini bank accounts, getting such men is easy in the Gulf, and making sure they don't miss, still easier.

We went out and walked along the beach away from the habitats. There was a lot of rubbish, roofs of huts, windows, a car or two rolled over, sheets of iron and bits of placards blown out from a half a mile or more inland. There was nobody about. No clearing had started in case Gertie came back, as she had twice before. She was still houri-ing around in the Gulf and the predictors were not sure what would happen next.

'You must take me seriously,' she said.

'Believe me, darling, I'm dead serious. Where is he now?'

'He went down-town, drinking. He'll wind up finding somebody who wants a drop. He went with Harz.'

'That German has a poker face at all times, playing or no,' I said.

I thought of the four of them. Gordon was a Scot from Pittsburgh, who had wound up in steel. Gorse had oil in Texas. Harz was in chemicals in the Ruhr. Pat Mancini was an Irish-Italian from Hackney who had got his own back for a bad start by cheating everybody since. He had floated around in electronics, buying this firm, selling out quick, getting another and so on. I suspected he was a kiteflier to begin with, then the City moneylenders got the measure of him and he had had a spare million, or several, to get hold of some other firms. He had no scruples. Nor had the other three. You can't make a million with a heart like a soft-shelled crab. It takes a hide like a brontosaurus.

Again I wondered if the cable meant money.

Then I wondered what Pat Mancini was doing.

'For Pete's sake!' she said suddenly angry. 'Aren't you worried?'

'What can we do?' I said, facing her. 'Get a plane out? I know a small Auster that happened to miss everything. God knows how, but it did.'

'Fly off — with the hurricane still around?'

'What's a hurricane? It's better than being shot in the back. Besides, it doesn't *have* to come up on us. The shot does.'

The chit-chat was light, but the meaning behind it was not. I was still uncertain whether this threat was some little game she was playing, for she was all times playful, but every time I thought of Mancini, my ideas got chilled.

He was the kind of bastard who would do it.

'He doesn't love you,' I said.

She laughed then.

'He never did. I was a piece of his personal glory. Something to hang the beads on. Ugly men like to have beautiful wives. I'm that, if nothing else.'

'But you loved him to marry him?'

'Man, I was eighteen, run away to the stage, failed and was considering the bed-to-bed routine when he turned up a Rolls and all the Irish-Italian romantic blarney ever invented. I didn't know he stays up at night when he's drunk and rehearses it all over. I always know when some other tart has turned up in his life. He actually tapes the routine and learns it from that.' She laughed. It wasn't too hard a sound.

'So you could have shed him before?' I said.

She looked me hard in the eye.

'There's me, and the things I've got now. And there's him, and he thinks of me as part of his goods, and what he's got doesn't get away. He had Peter Gay shot outside a club in Soho. Nobody was ever caught. They were hired killers and had no motive anybody would spot. He thought Peter was my lover. He wasn't. It was a wrong guess, but Peter Gay died.' Her hard look died and she smiled a little. 'So you see, I'm worried.'

'Just worrying's no good,' I said.

'Something has to be done. How long does it take him to get drunk?'

'All day. He's well run-in.'

'So we should have a while to consider,' I said. 'What have you in mind? I'm not going to murder him. Besides, he might have fixed up to have us done before I got him, I haven't got a million to square the police. The only thing for safety is to go while he's not looking.'

'He'd follow.'

'He might not know where to follow?'

'And what way is there but the boat? The airlines won't start up again till the hurricane's dead.'

'There's that Auster,' I said. 'I know Barney. He's chief of the flying club.'

'That's an idiot idea.'

'It's the only way. Or stay and get shot.'

Her eyes narrowed.

'Why do you carry a gun?' she asked quickly.

'I'm a licensed member of a pistol club. I go round shooting — at targets. I have some very fine pistols at home. This one is a kind of general purpose thirty-eight. Targets or otherwise.'

13

'You weren't frightened you might have to use it?'

'I'm always frightened of that.'

She turned and started to beat in from the beach. Once in amongst the trees, partly stripped and tattered though they were now, she clearly felt easier.

'It's so easy to see along the beach with glasses,' she said.

They all had houses, the Four Rich Men, and each house had servants, and all servants have lots of eyes. There is a hot little sideline in blackmail in these playgrounds, and eyes are always filling in blanks for the pressure operators.

It was a wonder to me I hadn't been approached already. We hadn't been particularly careful. Of all the careless raptures I had known this had been the one caring least for the outsider.

Remembering it, I wanted to go all through it again, as if that might magically disperse all surrounding difficulties.

I was at this time still unsure of the gravity of our situation, even though I remembered the reports of Peter Gay being shot outside a club.

That easy, sophisticated, throw-it-away grace she had still stuck to her as if, deep down, she was ashamed to be frightened of somebody.

It didn't impress me as it should have done. Also, after the strain of Gertie, I was in a mood to relax and rest out from the worry of sudden death.

★　★　★

I put my face under the yard wide brim of her hat and kissed her. The hat pushed off and slid down her back and hung there over my arms. We stayed a little while like it for The Chemical is hard to damp down.

At the end she kept hold of my arms.

'We've got to go,' she said urgent at last. 'He'll kill us. It's the only thing that will satisfy him now. You won't believe it, but he enjoys it. He likes people to suffer and squirm so that he can watch. He'd stick you to the wall with a pin if he could, and watch you die there.'

The old shell of sophistication was

suddenly cracked and broken away. She was real, as real as she was in all passion.

It was the first time I saw the blaze of the true situation and the fear of it broke into me like water breaking a dam.

Loving her had been splendid, wonderful, exciting. But all the time we had been together, Pat Mancini had been playing poker. Then suddenly he had invited me into the game. For what, now, could that have been?

To get to know me better, clean me out, skin me before I was skewered.

'A boat,' she said quickly. 'We could take one of the boats.'

'But then they could use the Auster and spot us easily. No, the plane is the best.'

'The plane's just mad! You might as well not go at all! Just stay and be shot!'

'Have more faith,' I said. 'And anyhow, don't let anybody start chasing too soon. We must be innocent to begin with. Back to the bar. So long as we're there, the followers will think they needn't watch too hard. I don't like it out here.' I looked round, through the cane trees to the golden beach, then back towards the blazing flowers running in towards the golf course. 'Too many trees.'

We walked back to the beach. I explained it was important to act as if we didn't suspect Pat or anybody he might be hiring. She played up well. It was handy she had learned about acting, here and there.

Walking back, she left me often to go over near the sea and walk in the shallow edge.

Back in the bar I ordered more drinks.

'How's the phone, Joey?' I said.

'All right now, mass. Okay, okay. Down below it's all down, but here okay to the radio station. You want long?'

Some people came in the end of the bar.

'Just give it to me, Joey.'

He slammed the phone on the bar and pushed it across at me. There was a lot of sand glittering on his usually spotless counter. I put in the personal call to Bill Solstice. It would catch him after lunch, I hoped.

A few more people came in. They were all talking about their personal Gertie

17

experiences, and laughing now, though I saw a frequent glance out towards the veranda and the sea.

The sky was a bit brassy. Gertie was not very far away. The fans weren't working. The juice lines were still down. I thought Joey would run out of ice, soon. Jo just sat there, staring over her drink at a PanAm calendar. The little groups in the bar often stopped talking to drink. There were too many pauses.

They were waiting for something.

Somebody got a weather flash on a transistor. Gertie was still moving, but had changed direction twice in twelve hours and they couldn't pin where she was going. She might stay still, but she had a long way to go before she wandered into the Atlantic and blew out.

It was very still out there on the beach, and the sun was not so bright, but hazed somehow.

The call came through quickly, not twenty minutes from take-off, which was good in the circumstances.

'Jonathan Blake here in sunny Albango Bay,' I said.

'Lucky you, Johnny. Lucky all through. You got the wire?'

'This morning. It was lucky. We're almost blown out. Well, what is this? Dare I come back?'

'You should. You're in the rich. Ever heard of a Roger Blake?'

'I think there was a cousin that way named.'

'There was. He's dead. The estate's big. You'd better come home, Jon Blake. It's most important.'

'Is there any cash immediately available? I've been playing poker. Short on traveller's cheques.'

'We'll fix it. Just say what you want.'

It was difficult to say. I didn't know where I would be in a couple of hours' time, and I didn't want duns hanging on the Auster tail.

'Cable five hundred to the hotel here,' I said.

She touched my knee.

'I can fix money. Don't worry about that,' she whispered.

'When'll you be back?' Solstice said.

'Soon as. What sort of stuff is this?'

'All kinds. Not cash, but convertible. Readily. You needn't worry any more.'

'Can you hear me clearly?' I cupped my hand over the mike.

'Perfectly.'

'Don't believe anything unless you see my body. Demand to see it. You get that?'

There was a pause and a hiss.

'Look, what are you up to now? You don't need anything! Just come home.'

'I'm the man giving the instructions. I'll be home soon as I can, but if you hear anything, demand to see. I'll feel better if you say yes.'

He said yes. It was a pained, incredulous sound.

'For God's sake behave,' he said at last.

'Always,' I said, uncupping. 'Keep expecting me.'

When I rang off and pushed the phone away I saw her looking at me very oddly.

'I want to get out of here now,' she said very quietly.

'Okay.'

Joey beamed like a car front as we slipped off the stools and went out. This time we went down into the car park.

There was a lot of rubbish about, but from the road we could hear clearance trucks banging and clattering and roaring as stuff was thrown on to their open backs.

She had a Moke there, a little automated skate Pat usually used to go to the golf course, and around it, if he felt like that. It was his favourite drunk wagon.

'He walked downtown?' I said.

'You couldn't drive there, early on.' She was tense and terse as well. She was suddenly anxious to get out of the hotel and its yard.

We got in — or on the vehicle. She started up and we skated out into the road under the trees.

'I hate hibiscus,' she said.

'What else?' I said. 'Somebody in the bar?'

'What was that call?'

'To my solicitors.'

'It was tapped.'

'How do you know?'

'There was a girl and a man at the far end of the bar.

She was very dark and he light — German-looking.'

'I saw — afterwards.'

'When you had the phone he went out and across the vestibule into the office. She just waited. When you finished he came back, and she looked at you.'

'I thought it was my charm. You're needling me.'

It was one thing to talk rubbish, another to think what she meant. If the call had been tapped, what was it to anyone else? I'd come into something. It wasn't hurting anybody, specially nobody on that island.

'I just said I would be home when I could,' I told her. 'How could that help?'

'Do you know those two?' she said.

'I've seen them about. Forget where.'

'She got Gorse. He had to pay her more than something. She's a playground pirate.'

'Why does she need me?'

'Gorse did something. Fixed her somehow. The blond man's her friend, or pimp. He gets rich women.'

'They should do well.' I said. 'What

happened to spike the business? Gorse?'

'Something Gorse did. He's mean as hell, but he paid up at a start. Then he got her fixed somehow. Shouldn't be surprised if he didn't blackmail her. That's the sort of game he likes. Extremely strip poker. I don't know what he did to her, but I know what they do together. If she looked at you — watch it! I know that much.'

'She won't get me in bed with a camera,' I said.

We were heading for the airfield. Mel Barney ran it. An Australian I met in Malaya during the Commie war. He was flying transports in the R.A.A.F. He packed in and got a job out on the island, Chief Flying Instructor to the club. He found there was a lot of rich tipping going on. Gradually he bought a half-dozen hire and sporting light planes. At this time, he was doing well and used a lot of cigars. The women liked him to teach them flying. He bullied the hell out of them.

We were on the country road between the flowers with telegraph posts and light wires lurching all over the sky. There are

23

too many flowers. The country looked overpainted.

Like the girl.

'What names?' I said.

'The man's Karl Muck.'

'Splendid.'

'Pronounced Mook, naturally. The girl's called Oleander.'

'You joke?'

'No, that's it. And nothing else known, as far as names go. She has been up twice on suspected murder charges, and he once, with her. One of his lady clients was found dead in an hotel in Miami, but nothing could be fixed on him. Not even some of the missing jewellery.'

'A real couple of playground pro's,' I said. 'But then, wealth breeds fleas. What are you stopping for?'

She pulled the skate in against the flowers and the wires trailing in amongst them. A Land-Rover went screaming by with some official title painted on it.

She looked across to the sky over the sea. It was getting very coppery now, and everything was still as death. Again I got that nervous catch in my stomach, the catch of apprehension.

'What are you proposing to do?' she said, and she sounded hard.

'Get the plane, fly off. Outwardly, the pleasure flip. It's got to look like an accident.'

She jerked with fear and her eyes opened a moment before she got control.

'Look like an accident!' she snapped. 'It bloody well will be if you take off in this!'

'Then they'll think we're lost. Finis. Sad end. Pat screaming with remorse — '

'You don't make me laugh!'

'Why not? It's what I'm going to do. You don't want to stay, do you?' I looked at her.

'You're a hard bastard in your quiet little way, aren't you?'

'Don't spit at me. Think of me as the knight gallant, saving you from a death worse than fate — ' I grabbed her wrist and made it hurt a bit. 'We have to do this. It happens to be true I wouldn't let you stay. He'd do you, that husband of yours. I believe that. We took a risk when we started this. That means we have to go on taking risks. If we go and come down

25

in the sea where we don't mean to, what does it matter? Staying here we're waiting for the same sort of thing. I can't stand waiting. Must move. That's me. But he who keeps moving is harder to hit.'

She grabbed me round the neck and we kissed. It was a daft and dangerous thing to do, but at the time it seemed absolutely essential. We hung on for a while after, too, just hugging.

We were hugging when a little Ford went by, throwing up petals and leaves thrown all over the road. We hadn't heard it. It went on without slackening pace.

She pushed me away when the wheels went by, brushing and wittering on the leaves and stuff.

'Harz,' she said, staring after the little car. 'That's his! That tiger in the window. Harz!'

I cursed, but within. The feeling I had then was that she had gone through a good deal more tension than she made out, and that if I showed more of it, she'd feel twice as bad.

As we started off again, I remembered the dark, brooding face of Mancini, rolling a cigar between his teeth from one side of his slit to the other, his squat fingers tight on the cards. He wouldn't let them go. He wouldn't let her go, unless he sent her himself.

The memory was shaking. I don't know why. I hadn't felt it during the game, just formed the idea he felt a lot he didn't show. Whenever he had lost he had shown his teeth, like a pleased tiger.

The airfield looked a mess. The beautiful flowers and general decor had been tattered and shattered and some of the facings of the buildings torn off, revealing the tawdry underneath.

Mel Barney's offices were on the right of the entrance, a group of long low huts, and he had three of the old nissen type hangars. One had withstood Gertie so far, and the Auster stood with perky, up-poking nose inside it, a bag over her Gipsy engine.

Round about there was a Piper on its back, an old Tiger (Mel's favourite stunter), on one wheel, fabric hanging limp from a shattered wing. There was nobody about. Reclamation hadn't begun.

Jo stopped the Moke, but I made her go on again round the end of the hut building where the car wouldn't be seen from the road. It would be located in the end, but there was no point in waving flags to lead the searchers to us.

We got out, and went along the veranda by the office doors until we came to one marked 'C.F.I. Mel Barney, Sq. Ldr., R.A.A.F.'

I knocked and heard Mel say. 'Come in, sport.'

I opened the door and let her by me. We went in and I shut the door.

Mel was sitting on his desk swinging a leg, looking at us askance.

He had an automatic in his hand, a Mauser, and it pointed at me.

'Stand over there, sport,' he said. 'Just unluckily, I can't call the cops, because the line's down, but we can wait.'

2

Mel Barney was a handsome sort of fellow in a tanned, dried sort of way. He had very light coloured eyes and as they fixed on me they seemed to have boring qualities.

The gun he held was very steady. He had an arm across his knee as he sat on the desk and his gun wrist rested across it.

Jo looked back at me, and for the first time I saw a look of real fear in her eyes. Whether she expected me to show a similar anxiety I don't know, but when surprised I'm all right. My inner make-up responds to the sudden demands of the moment. It's when it has to wait it frays away.

'Aren't you going to offer us a drink, sport?' I said, and sat down in one of his wicker arm-chairs. I grinned at him and saw the gun muzzle follow me down until I had sat firmly in the chair.

'What's the name, sport?' he said, coolly.

'Don't say you don't know me,' I said.

He looked at Jo then nodded to a cigarette box.

'Help yourself to a smoke, dear,' he said. 'That'll give him time to remember.'

His attitude ceased to shock. it was puzzling now. He watched me, but I watched him just as sharply. We tried to see into each other, and I could see the mists of doubt begin to shade his penetrating stare.

'Sure you look like him,' he said.

'I am him,' I said. 'Jonathan Blake.'

He laughed suddenly.

'Maybe I have news for you, depending on which one you arc, sport,' hc said. 'Right now there's two such Blakes. I have a warning.'

'Two?' I just stared.

'Yay, sure, two,' he said. 'You wouldn't have seen the other if you're the right. If you're the left, I'm not wasting my time. Crack on, then. *Prove*.'

The way he said it was nasty, and I knew him well enough to remember he was hard, almost without scruples when it came to a job that had to be done. I felt glad I was me. I wished I could prove it easily.

In my mind I went through some of the places we had known together in Malaya while he just sat, watching me. Then suddenly I had it.

'Remember the two Chinese Janes?' I said. 'The ones who turned out to be spies? That knifing?'

I undid my shirt and pushed it aside, turning so he could see the back of my left shoulder. Jo stared at me with a tense frown on her face.

Behind me, Mel took a deep, slow breath. I felt his touch on my skin as he tried to see if the scar rubbed off.

'Yay,' he said. His voice drew away behind me and I turned back.

He laid the gun on the desk.

'Have a drink, sports,' he said.

He watched Jo as he poured. He had seen her before, of course. It's a very small society on these islands, and if you are white and seem to have money you're bound to meet.

There was a cowardly relief spreading through me as I did my shirt up again.

'What come you for, then, cobber?' he said. He misplaced his words with some idea of irony, perhaps, or a refusal to accept the rules, but it made him very easy to imitate. I had been fooled once on a phone in Singapore.

'I wish to hire an aircraft,' I said, and smiled, I hoped, benevolently.

I thought he would run off the end, go mad, scream with hysterical laughter, or perhaps just spit. I was surprised when he didn't. He just went on handing us glasses. In fact, he looked thoughtful.

'There is but one aircraft serviceable,' he said, and raised his glass. 'Mud, matey.' He drank as if it were some kind of mouthwash, swilling it round his teeeth before he swallowed it. 'Why wish you to flug in these here edgy conditions?'

'It's calm enough,' I said.

'Oh, aye,' he said. 'As of now.' He was still thoughtful. He was actually considering the proposition. It was incredible. 'Of my six planes five are out.'

'Bad time for the insurance boys,' I said.

His light eyes drifted to Jo, and almost warmed up a little as he watched her.

'Yay, yay,' he said. 'I would have to D.I. it, me personally.' He looked from her to me. 'Where do you bung for?'

'Over to Flamingo Bay.' I said. 'Just a trip to get the sensation of moving air.'

It took some callousness to sit there grinning at him, knowing I intended to lose the aircraft for him. I was going on over Flamingo Bay, right over. And whether Gertie got us or not, the Auster was going to sink in the open sea.

It was not until I sat coldly foreseeing my full plan that I realised it was based on a pure, cold fear of being shot in the back by Pat's hirelings. Not only me, but Jo as well. It was as if our deaths were a dead cert if we stayed any longer on this island. I hadn't admitted this certainty in the front of my mind, but my thoughts proved it was set firmly in the back of it.

'You just want for the flug, then?' he said, sitting back in his chair.

'Just for the flug,' I said.

'If that goes,' he said sitting forward suddenly, 'then I could give you an aim, sport. You could do an errand for me. Practice landing east of the bay. There's a wee strip there.' He opened a drawer in his desk. He seemed quite matter of fact, but I sensed some kind of tension in him. 'The lines being kaput, matey, I canna say that this won't be there.'

He wagged a leather wallet as if beating time with it.

'What is it?' Jo said.

'It is some gen I promised to send, dearest cock,' he said. He smiled but there was no humour in his eyes. 'I was thinking of getting a message through. but not now you're here. For myself, sport, I have to stay here. There is the insurance assessor man on his way. I must be around to fill in all the lies. Three of my planes were sold up, anyway. I only got 'em to fly with sticky tape.'

He was drunk.

The fact struck me suddenly, and only because I had known him well in the past. Usually, he showed no normal sign even when the booze was almost running out of his ears, but if you knew him well you would begin to recognise a laziness in his eyes and in the thought behind his speech.

'Well,' he said, 'you do this little thing for me, sport? It comes under flying practice. No charge.'

'You book me out as for pleasure,' I said firmly. 'Passenger, Mrs. Josephine Mancini.'

'Surely, sport, san fairy,' he said and pushed the book across to me. 'You fill in. I'll sign. I'll sign for the D.I., too. Save time.'

'Yes,' I said. 'Do that, too.'

Signing for the Daily Inspection without having done the job, would be a fair reason for us to fall in the sea.

The D.I. is an inspection of the engine and airframe to ensure everything is in order, and has to be done by a qualified man or men. It also includes filling up with gas and oil and anything else needed. All these items are then written in the form belonging to the aircraft, signed for by the qualified man, and signed for by the pilot as acceptance that the machine is fit to fly.

If Mel just signed without doing

anything, it would help the mystery of our disappearance.

The idea of this disappearance did not shock me then as it does now. My ideas seemed to have swollen with the association of a rich callousness, rife on the island. Chucking away an aircraft just didn't count against the possibility of getting murdered.

All along I had few qualms about that side of it as far as Mel was concerned, because he was insured to the hilt.

I filled in the book and he initialled it. I had filled in the destination as Flamingo Bay. As I did that I thought of taking off from the strip there and heading out and out over the sea —

Then suddenly the heady notion came to me that I was rich, like the other people, like Mancini and his pals. All of a sudden it didn't matter if I threw away a plane. I could buy Mel another without waiting for the insurance to pay up.

The fact was, the cable from London had jerked me into a world that had never existed before. All my normal view of things had slipped sideways. I had blown big-headed with sudden wealth and the illusion of power.

Perhaps it had given me the idea that I didn't have to stay and fight any more. I could afford to run away.

'The wallet,' Mel said. He slipped some rubber bands round it to hold it shut. 'All you do is land. Somebody will come and take it from you.'

'They'll be expecting me?'

'No, but there's always somebody there when any aircraft gets near,' he said dryly. 'You might say you'll be covered as soon as you land. Friendliwise.'

He stood up and gave me the wallet across the desk.

'Do I get anything signed for it?'

'No, you just hand over and take straight off.'

'They'll know the plane?'

'Sure enough.'

He went to the door and opened it for us.

It was dead calm outside. The sky was brassier than before. The heat was like something crowding in on you, cotton wool, suffocating. Mel leant against a veranda post and gazed upwards through a torn piece of the veranda roof.

'She's coming back, sport. You'd better wait.'

I looked round the empty field.

'Where's everybody?' I said.

'Home. Clearing up.'

The stillness was the atmosphere of a dream.

'She'll go out this time, right out over the ocean. I heard a weather flash. The man said.'

He did not seem to be convinced by me, but he didn't seem to care much, either. I reckoned he was worried, and he was drunk because of that. I would have said, on guess, that Mel was the type never to worry about anything, but you can't tell what suddenly comes up behind a man.

Jo had been very quiet all the time, hardly spoken a word. Perhaps she realised early he wouldn't have listened if she had said something. He was too far out on some trouble.

She gave me a look.

'I'll wait for you,' she said.

'Fine,' I said.

Mel and I walked off towards the old blister hangar. Away in the trees some birds started screaming. I wondered why they didn't sing, like they did at home. But this kind of rich nature was violent, the colours, the sounds — and the storms.

And the kind of people who came here. They bought violence, created it with money. They bought a way out of law, too. I have been wrong side of the law fence before now, and it has seemed fair, because I always knew which side the law was on. I knew where to look. Here, you didn't. Mancini and his friends could buy it up and put it which side they liked.

Mel walked slowly over the grass. I fretted to get on to the nosebagged plane.

'What's this about my double?' I said.

He frowned at the distance.

'I got the wire about a half-hour before you turned up,' he said.

'Who gave it?'

'Police patrol. He was out on missing persons check. There's been a bomb of damage. They keep looking, times like

39

this.' He was moody and depressed, just throwing the words away.

'Why should you have to look out for my double?'

'Case of a break,' he said. 'They think this cobber might try and do the bunk by flippage.' He scratched his jaw. 'I never saw another mug like yours in all my life.'

'Funny I didn't see him. Nobody's left the island for days.'

'Yay, yay,' he said.

We got to the plane. He unfastened the nosebag.

'What's eating you, Mel?'

He looked at me. The prop was almost between us, like some kind of lethal chopper. I thought he was going to open up, but he lost tension and went on getting the bag off.

A car went slowly by on the road beyond the flowered bushes. I was nervous, then. If any car went slowly on that island it was like a sore thumb and seemed to mean trouble.

So I felt.

★ ★ ★

He got the bag off, upped the cowling and looked in at the engine. He wasn't doing anything. Just stopping me talking. I got in the cabin and tested the controls. He went round on the outside, watching them flap, sometimes shoving them with his hand. He was thinking, thinking, but not about aeroplanes.

He came round and stood looking in at the cabin, his light eyes narrowed.

'That China girl who stabbed you,' he said.

'I often wonder if she meant it,' I said.

'No. She missed. She meant to have you right through your old blood pump. They don't show what they're thinking. Dead pans. This popsie's Mancini's bride?'

He cocked his head.

'Yes.' I watched him.

'She'll do the China on you,' he said. 'Get her off your back.'

For a moment his words struck a chill in me, but if there was one thing I wasn't frightened of just then it was Jo.

It was about the only thing. The slow movement, the still air and the dull, waiting sky were adding up to a nervous twist.

'Can't,' I said, reaching for the switches. 'I'm going to wind up the elastic.'

'Okay,' he said and walked backwards along the trailing edge of the wing, watching me all the time.

★   ★   ★

The engine started all right. We rolled out on to the grass and let it warm up. He just stood there, holding a wingtip with one hand, staring down, watching the grass flatten in the slipstream.

I'd never seen anyone so changed as he was. He was so depressed he almost wasn't there.

When she was hot enough I switched off and got out on to the grass. Beyond the flowers the car went slowly by again. It must be the same one, I thought. There couldn't be two cars going slowly on that island.

Over at the offices I saw Jo come out on to the veranda, hesitate, looking over towards us, then go round the end to the Moke. She got something out of it, when her attention was attracted by the slow car, too.

It seemed to stop altogether, but the engine still hissed on. Then it picked up again. Jo could see between the bushes. She straightened up from the little truck and came towards us. The sound of the car faded along the road.

'It's the Harz car again,' she said, coming up.

'It went by just now. That's three times,' I said. 'What's it on — patrol?'

'Are we going?' she said abruptly.

'Yes.'

I looked at Mel. He was looking at me, almost as if he would let himself go and tell me what was on his mind. But his eyes flicked to Jo, and he bit it all back.

She got into the plane. I looked at Mel again, but he hardened. His lean jaw bit hard and I saw his teeth clenched together.

'Better run her up,' he said.

I got in and started again. There was no drop in revs when tested at full power, and I throttled back again and made sure the door was fast. He just stood there, hanging on the wingtip, staring towards us.

Then he let go and put his thumb up. I opened up and he fell behind. There wasn't any wind. I just took off straight ahead.

We lifted after a short run and at two hundred feet I made a starboard climbing turn, bringing us over the road. Way up it I saw the little grey Ford. It was stopped under the trees by a lot of broken wire snaking on the road.

As we swung over, the car door opened and a man got out. He put a pair of field glasses to his eyes. I tipped the plane up, making the bank steeper so he could see only our belly before we slipped out of his sight over the trees.

'Who was that?' I said.

'With a hat on and binocks to his face — I couldn't tell.' She was sharp, tense. 'What's the matter with your friend?'

'My friend has the weltschmerz,' I said. 'Perhaps he has a hangover.'

'There's something wrong down there,' she said.

I levelled out at five hundred. I didn't particularly want to get any higher. The higher you go, the more people can see you, and I didn't want to be seen while still over the island.

Over the sea, the sky was still a weird yellow colour, but the water was millpond still. The wreckage on the beach looked like litter paper after a Bank Holiday. Away in the west the rich white houses of the millionaires peeped from their still luxurious herbage. We couldn't see the damage from the distance we were.

'Is he a spy?'

'Who? Barney? For the lord's sake, what made you say a thing like that?'

'There was some talk a while ago that he was in with Pachmann.'

'Who's Pachmann?'

She laughed.

'Pachmann knows everybody, but nobody knows Pachmann.'

'Where does he hang out?'

'He has a private island, thirty miles out.'

'Not Shark Island?'

'Yes. Barney runs a small air service for Shark Island.'

'Are you meaning Pachmann is some sort of an international operative?'

'I think he runs an international service of information.'

'A kind of subliminal news agency?'

'As you say.'

'I heard of Shark Island as a big place for parties, big fishing, boar hunting and such, but not of Pachmann.'

'Pachmann's the kind everybody likes to call by his Christian name in public. So it's always Gabriel.'

'Ah! Yes. Now that's a familiar.'

I settled on a compass course for Flamingo Bay and set the direction indicator to it.

'But surely Mel doesn't have to be an agent to fly for Gabriel Pachmann? He'd be a fool if he didn't. He's in flying for money. It costs a lot of upkeep these days.'

She stared out of her window over the sea.

'It was just an idea,' she said. 'It's easy to get involved in this part of the world.'

I looked at her and thought what truth she spoke. The tension in me had eased with getting off the ground, and pounding on over the forest towards Flamingo Bay, I began to think a bit more calmly about what was going on.

The days with Gertie had been a strain. You don't go about being sporadically bashed and whipped by mad, uncontrollable elements without losing a bit of self-confidence. All right, perhaps, when you're used to it, but though I had seen many storms in my travels, I had never been in such a riptearing bombardment of sheer terror as Gertie had provided.

To come out of it and find oneself likely to be shot in the back was mild by comparison, but it did mean no easing of tension, and I was fed up with suspense by then.

The news of a small fortune had been a shock, a jolt, but it had seemed to put another twist on the screw because, mortally, it seemed desperately important to find out what I really had, what sort of relief from urgent life I could expect.

In short, during that day, I was not myself. I was an overwound clock spring and the pep-up from London had just made it jangle.

As I watched the instruments I remembered what Mel had said about the China girl.

Then I realised that nobody had threatened me but Jo.

She had said Pat was on the warpath. She had said he had gone downtown to find a murderer or two. But then, racing above the tree carpet in the clear, hot air, the whole picture became suddenly sharp and clear.

Had I believed too much of what she'd said?

At any other time I would have been more sure of myself, but Gertie with her noise and terror and sleep-killing had made all the difference in the world to my outlook.

'There are clouds on the horizon,' she said. 'Over the sea. Look!'

It was indistinct. It was some kind of dark mess and it seemed to be rising into the sky.

It was Gertie coming back.

'How long to Flamingo Bay?' she said.

'Thirty minutes.'

'She travels a long way in a half-hour,' Jo said. 'Gertie, I mean.'

'I know what you mean.'

'We're not going away from it?'

'We're running alongside, you might say, judging from the position of the muck.'

'It seems to be swelling. Like it did on Tuesday.'

'I can't think what's the matter with Gertie,' I said, re-checking the direction indicator. 'She won't go. The met men keep saying she will, but she goes on spinning like some weary old top that won't fall down.'

'I distrust you when you're flippant.'

We were getting a lot of bumps off the forest, where it kept breaking into sandy open bits. Away to starboard the great mass of the mountain stood like a Greek archbishop's hat, a silent monument against the brassy, waiting sky. I had a momentary nightmare vision of Gertie whipping by it in a mass of black sulphur and smoke and then passing and leaving no mountain at all.

I watched the forest and the mops of the tree tops. They were moving slightly now.

The stillness was over. The wind was moving down there.

Checking our drift, I reckoned it was rising ten to fifteen miles an hour across us. I steered into it a couple of degrees and we began to crab on our way where before we had been heading direct.

As the minutes passed, the bumpiness got worse and I steered three more degrees into the rising wind.

It was all right so far, for the speed of the wind was rising steadily and roughly on our port beam. Soon with the great rising mess of the hurricane in the far sky, the air would begin to racket around in all directions, and suddenly I agreed with my coward's ego that it would be best to be down before Gertie got here.

The bumps were getting so that we fell a lot and then were jumped up a lot. I went up to twelve hundred. It wasn't any smoother but there was more room to lose height when the bumps got worse.

'How long now?' she said.

'Damn! you can add up, can't you?'

After a while she said, 'That engine sounds funny.'

I said, 'It can afford to. It's the only one we've got.'

The drift was increasing fast. I nosed into wind again.

We were really crabbing now. The next time she asked how long, I gave her my guess.

'We must be going slower.'

'Surely we are,' I said. 'The more we head to the wind the less speed we make forward. Just plain maths.'

It was getting rough then, and the smear of Gertie was big on the horizon.

'We ought to put down somewhere,' she said.

She was tensed up now. Bumping around in an aircraft with a storm about is a sure way to give anyone an injection of suspense value.

'We're putting down at Flamingo Bay,' I said.

'And staying,' she said.

'We'll see what the weather's like.'

'Are you crazy? Look over there.'

51

'Look ahead. We're only ten minutes off.'

Her edginess was increasing with the bucketing. We crabbed more and more along the track to Flamingo Bay. Below us the tree tops were beaten into light waves by the rising wind, but still it was keeping to one direction.

Gertie must still have been some distance off then.

My earlier determination to use the hurricane edge as a part excuse to vanish had now receded. Taking risks is all right if you feel you'll live after. But if you don't, there's no point to it.

On the port beam the dirty mess in the sky was piling very high now, so high it seemed to be leaning over the sky to come nearly over the top of us. There was day on the starboard and increasing night on the port.

'There's the bay!' she said, pointing ahead.

She rolled against me with a sudden drop of the starboard wing.

'Fix your strap,' I said. 'It'll be rougher nearer the ground.'

By then I had gone up to two thousand to leave more room and perhaps to get a little smoother. The beating of the trees below showed how rough it was getting down there.

'Suppose — ' she said, and stopped.

'Suppose what?'

I had the feeling I knew what she was going to say, and I was right.

'Suppose the strip doesn't point the right way,' she said.

'We'll manage,' I said.

Ahead of us the water in the bay looked smooth still, but outside the horn of the headland the white horses were creaming up in slow motion.

With three miles to go for the beach, I should have spotted the strip, but I saw nothing at all. It looked as if the trees went right to the beach.

The wind then was beating roughly in from the headland, where the beach faded into cliffs. That meant the only beach that could be landed on was now almost dead cross wind, and the wind, judging from our bucketing about, must have been gusting to fifty or sixty knots.

I couldn't say I had been caught out by the speed of the hurricane's approach. I had just been a fool to underestimate it. Even then it seemed to me to be coming up much quicker than on its previous visits.

'Can we get down on the beach?' she said.

'Not with this wind across us and gusting. We'd stick a wing in. Unless the beach is deep enough to get into the wind. Even then it'll be a weary experience.'

We were over the beach then. I lost height and made a big circle, looking down to spot the best chance of a landing.

It was getting dark, not with night, but with the great black mass of the shadow reaching over us. We were being beaten about hard then, like keep on hitting bricks underneath. The airframe seemed to grunt and snap with the increasing thumps.

'There's a light!' she gasped out. 'Over there, look!'

There was a light all right. It was an

Aldis lamp, signalling.

'Come in,' it flashed slowly.

'They think it's Mel,' I said, and tightened my circle.

I saw the strip. Of all things it was cut in the trees, and it looked just right to drive a Mini along. I headed into the wind with about twenty degrees off the main blow — that is if one could still judge the direction of the blow. It was getting so rough I felt it might start to turn before we got down.

I did a run along the top of the strip. We had to crab so much it seemed we were almost running along it broadside.

'Can you do it?' she said.

'I can do it,' I said.

Which was true. I could do it any day. It was just this particular day that it was doubtful, and that wasn't due to me.

I made a tight turn at the end, and we ran back alongside the strip at five hundred feet and going down with a lot of engine.

The wind behind us shoved us along at a spanking pace. I turned tightly at the end, losing height and heading in for the strip cut in the forest.

We jumped and swung about, and it was hell holding the light plane on to the approach line.

'Can you do it?' she shouted, for the wind was roaring around us now.

'Just hold tight!' I shouted back.

It was as we came down towards the strip that the bullet hole suddenly appeared in the perspex window at my side.

3

I had at that time my hand on the throttle and the other literally fighting the controls, which constantly tried to tear themselves away and submit to the terrifying buffeting.

Thus occupied, the full meaning of the bullet hole didn't register for a moment, one danger being very much like another. Then it came in with a bang.

'What's the matter?' Jo cried.

'We've been shot at!' I said. 'In the window and out the windscreen. Look! It must have been fired from close to!'

'We're too high — '

Both of us were misled in that first second of shock, by thinking the shot must have been fired from the ground, somewhere from down amongst the trees. The actual direction of the bullet didn't have meaning until the next instant. Then, lining up the two holes, the shot seemed to have come from our level and around five o'clock behind us.

Trying to keep the approach line was abandoned. I opened up and put her over in a steep turn, the wingtip on the port side seeming to mix in with the trees.

The whole of this took place in the weird copper dusk of the gathering tempest which distorted vision. Added to this the severity of the bucketing we were getting made it difficult to place the machine for a sharp look round.

As we turned, near the vertical, I looked up through the roof.

Another aircraft seemed on the point of crashing right into us. I saw the undercart and the nose suddenly heave themselves upwards and leapfrog, twisting into a turn as it went.

Our wings missed, but not by much. Once we had cleared each other and ripped off in different directions, the other plane seemed to shrink into the distance at a dizzy speed.

Then it turned, flat against the seascape, and came in again in pursuit.

'What on earth is it?' she cried. 'What are you going to do?'

'I don't know. It's somebody who thinks Mel's in here, and they mean to do him. There was a rifle sticking out of that starboard window. Shades of ancient wars!'

'We've got to get down!'

'Not here!' I shouted back.

We were cracking and roaring over the forest, seeming to crawl as we turned back into the searing wind.

The attacker was small against the smoky black of the whirlwind, but with the gale behind him he swelled up at a terrific rate, and against the darkness I saw the rifle spit two little, brilliant flashes.

He couldn't hit me except by a fluke, for we were both being thrown about by the wind, but in a situation of that surprising kind, you don't think of the enemy's chances, only your own.

I got down as low over the trees as I dared, being careful of a sudden bump putting us down into them.

He went by over the top of us. It looked like a Piper Cub to me. Almost as soon as he was over he turned sharply again, shrinking downwind in plan form until he straightened again and began to chase, head on.

There was no point in a position battle in a wind like this. There was a chance we had the edge on him for speed, with a bigger engine. I decided to run for it.

We roared out over the trees, passing across the landing strip, and lost height down over the beach. She took some holding, for the air kicks seemed to be bouncing up from the sand under us, shaking the thing almost out of my hands.

A momentary glance back towards the west showed the giant shape of Gertie blacking out the sky over there. We were still in the turbulent fringes of her gigantic spin.

The Piper was coming up over the trees in pursuit once more.

I zigzagged over the sea, heading for the towering breakers out beyond the headland.

'Where are you going?' she cried out.

'Away from him!' I said. 'What else can we do?'

I spared a moment from my tension to

admire her for her courage. After all, from her viewpoint, she was in the hands of a lunatic in a storm being fired at by other lunatics. Yet still she was in full command of herself.

'Keep your eyes on him!' I said.

'He's behind.'

'I know. How far?'

I opened up the curls of the zigzag so she could get a better look.

'I don't know. I'd think about a hundred yards.'

'God! As near as that! Can't be much in the speed, then.'

'But where are you going? It's open sea ahead!'

'And open graves behind,' I shouted back at her. 'Look, Gertie's back over the island. We can't go back to Barney's field. That geyser with the rifle is right behind. If we try and turn for that strip again, he can cut us off. Do you get that?'

'Yes, but there's nowhere ahead — '

'There's Shark Island, like you said.'

'Thirty miles! You're mad!'

'I didn't expect the rifle brigade to follow us up. We'd have just made it down to the strip, left alone. Now all we can do is run. Is he still there?'

'Sure he's still there!' She looked back through the roof as I banked in my turns.

'No nearer, no farther?'

'No.'

We came out over the open sea. Spray began to slide on the windscreen in moving sheets of water. The bumping got so I felt the wings would soon crack finally and fall off.

I had to get a bit more height. We were being thrown about too much to try and maintain desperate safety above the breakers. At times, indeed, they were so damn big it seemed we were going to fly right into the glassy green underside of each new wave.

I tried to keep the swinging compass somewhere on a rough — very rough course. The direction indicator was sliding its bearings through the slot, one way and then the other, but it made it possible for me to keep a rough heading away from the island and make for Shark.

Something must have shortened the distance between the planes, for we got a shot through the port wing which made a strip of canvas begin to tear back and whip on the wind. Much more of that and the rest would start loosening up.

'Is he nearer?' I shouted.

'No. Look, you can't — '

'He took a pot shot. Perhaps he's running out of the wish for sea travel.'

'Don't be so bloody funny!' she shouted.

'I mean it. My guess is he thinks we're just running. He'll drive us so far, then turn back. After all, he'll have to get down somewhere himself. Gertie won't leave him much more time.'

A shock suddenly thumped through the airframe.

'You hit the sea! Look, for heaven's sake turn back now. What's the use — '

'It wasn't the sea. Just a harder pocket than most.'

All the same, my fears were stringing up tight enough to fill in a tennis racket. At that height, in those conditions I began to get the old pilot's dread of the engine fading out. If it did even for an instant in this lot, we would be in the sea.

What looked like thirty foot breakers wasn't the sort of sea I'd planned to sink her in.

'They're climbing!' she said suddenly.

I gave myself some elevation, keeping a slow turn and then looked back. The Piper was climbing hard, and falling behind as it lost speed in the rise.

'He's changed his mind about something,' I said.

My throat was very dry and it hurt to speak. My impulsive nature makes me knock my knees after the main danger has gone by, and for a moment, watching the Piper shrink into the wild sky, I felt it had gone partially by.

'Are they giving up, then?' I said.

'They've got more sense than us.'

'I don't know about that.'

Looking back over the island, I thought that perhaps the pursuers had let this dedication to duty prevent them from looking back. Now they did, they saw a sky over the island that was terrifying.

The wild movements of the black columns of air in the distance persuaded me, at any rate, that any remote hope of getting back to the shore in a plane or a boat had been whipped away.

I understood now the pilot's feelings as he climbed into the copper sky and looked back at his last bridge burning in a wild fury of wind.

'He hasn't thought of Shark Island!' I yelled at her.

She let herself go a moment and covered her face in her hands. Looking back through the roof I saw the Piper high in the burning yellow sky, where the fringes of Gertie were edging up on him. He seemed to be still roughly on our heading, but getting remoter.

I was relieved to be able to get up off the floor. The waves didn't look so nightmarish from higher up.

She pulled herself together and uncovered her face.

'He's not turning back,' she said.

'No. I reckon he can see Shark Island from there.'

She laughed bitterly.

'So he'll be there too.'

'If Gertie doesn't overtake the both of us.'

My spirits rose somewhat at the feeling that the bumping was not quite so severe. Looking back over the stricken island we had left, it did seem that the risk we had taken might come off. Gertie appeared to be set over the land there, as if the new curve she was taking would draw away from us. But she was a long way from gone yet, and could, I remembered, swoop round another way.

It doesn't help to let sudden short relief bounce up one's optimism, but I can never help it. Which is why, my mother once told me, I always run into a mess.

But at that moment we did seem to have breathing space.

'They can watch and see where we go,' she said.

'They've got to go the same way,' I said. 'There isn't anywhere else.'

We bucketed on. The Piper seemed to be a long way up and two or three miles behind now.

'Who are they?' I said. 'Pat's men?'

But now there was a brief pause to think. I realised that plane had come from nowhere. There hadn't been anything in the sky with us when we'd come in above the strip.

'I don't think so,' she said. 'Nobody followed us. There was no other plane.'

'The only place they could have come from is up from the strip itself,' I said.

'But Barney said they would be expecting us there!'

'Well, they were!' I said. 'As soon as we droned up they took off and shot us in the rear.'

'You mean that Mel Barney sent you because he knew he was going to be — killed?'

She was horrified, and for a moment, so was I.

'No.' I said, shaking my mind back into perspective. 'No. That reception was meant to be a surprise for him. If it's any good guessing, I guess those geysers up there don't know he isn't in this kite. It'll be a surprise for them — if they're there when we get out.'

'I think it's getting calmer,' she said, suddenly.

It was just after that we fell fifty feet and shook about like a pea in a colander for minutes on end. Some undercurrent of air had got us and was shaking us by the ears.

I climbed up more. Jo didn't say anything about the weather after that. The horrid yellow sky was still ahead of us and the hurricane filled it behind us. We were not heading into sunshine. We were still, in fact, in the panic area, but not in such a rough bit as we had just come out of.

'If the storm's on again, Pat won't have time to do anything,' she said.

'He can sit wishing,' I said. 'That'll make it the more intense when he can move.'

'I don't think it matters so much about Pat now,' she said.

'The hell! why not?' I said. 'He still wants us killed! We wouldn't be here but for his objective!'

'What I mean is, I think Mel is a spy, or he's mixed up with Gabriel Pachmann somehow, and if that's so, we've been mixed up in it, too, and out here, things can get very exciting if somebody means to kill you.'

'There's too much money about,' I

said. 'Everybody gets aeroplanes and speedboats and killers and machine guns and personal size atom bombs just by snapping a few thousand dollars together. Back home the most you get is a Mini Cooper — stolen — and a second-hand forty-five.

'Unless, of course, you're robbing a train.'

She watched the distant Piper.

'It's rocking a lot,' she said.

'Gertie's coming up behind,' I said. 'She'll rock us more soon.'

The Piper had got so much height he had lost quite four miles on us. We had gone to about five hundred and the bumping was more manageable. All the same, the aircraft took constant, even violent, correction to keep it on the course.

It was a relief when suddenly we saw the smudge of Shark Island, about eight degrees off course ahead of us. For a moment relief made me feel that all was now well, all that remained was to get a hot bath and a comfortable sleep.

'You give up too soon,' my mother had

69

also said, many times.

According to the laws of geometry, velocities, angles and gravity, the Piper had but to nose down and open up and she would be right on top of us when the occasion demanded.

That part I ignored in the hope that the pilot and his rifler had changed tactics and taken on a watchdog, or shadow role.

★　★　★

'It's a very small island,' she said.

'It'll have to do.'

The smear of Gertie was coming up on our port horizon, getting ahead of us, like some encircling arm, meaning to gather us in. The island, a spot on the sea, was rocking up and down and across the windscreen as I fought the nose away from the persistent pushing and shoving of the wind.

The sea below was rough, streaming with horses, the waves a good deal bigger than they looked from five hundred feet.

'There must be a landing place there,' she said. 'Barney runs a service.'

'So you said. But just suppose these boys up behind us come from Gabriel, anyhow? What happens when we get down on the island?'

'But Barney was working in with GP. Gabriel wouldn't have had him shot.'

'If Gabriel is a big time news provider, his attitude might change overnight. Barney could know something.'

'What's in the wallet?'

As I looked at her I saw her face was firm, determined.

'I don't know.'

'What are you going to do with it now? The people you were to give it to are either going to kill you or they're dead already, down on that strip.'

'I am aware of the possibilities.'

'See what's in the wallet. Then we'll know where we stand.'

I hesitated. The island was growing bigger, a small, somehow menacing heap in the middle of a stormy yellow sea.

'It's a fair suggestion,' I said.

'Give it to me,' she said.

I got the wallet out of my pocket but stayed holding it a while.

'What's the matter?' she said quickly.

'I just don't like prying into his affairs.'

'He nearly got you shot!'

'He doesn't know.'

'Then why didn't he go himself?'

'He wanted to stay.' I remembered his story about waiting for the insurance assessor, and it was feeble and stupid. I didn't repeat it.

'He didn't want to be shot,' she said angrily. 'Why do you think he let you have the plane so easily? Have you thought of that?'

Twisting my neck I saw the Piper higher, even farther behind now. The black smudge in the sky was over him like a hellish canopy. We were about seven miles off Shark Island.

'Open the wallet, then,' I said.

She took off the rings and opened the leather folder. She looked into it, all the compartments, then she looked at me.

'There's nothing in it,' she said. 'Nothing at all!'

'There must be, somewhere. Look again!'

She looked again, practically turned it inside out.

'There's nothing in it,' she said again. 'It was a trap.'

'I've known Mel for years!' I shouted at her.

'What difference does that make? He's got in a mess and handed it to you. You can't blame him when you see the trouble they went to.' She indicated the distant Piper with the wallet, fierily contemptuous.

'It makes no difference,' I said. 'This is what I meant to do.'

'With them on your tail?'

'I don't know what this is about. Mel thought there was something in that wallet when he gave it to me. I'm not changing my mind on that.'

'He might have taken more care — for the sake of a dear old friend.'

'If you sneer at my friends I'll tip you out!' I said.

'I'll drag you with me.'

The engine spat, as if to join in the fight. It made us concentrate on the motor instead of ourselves. The steady rhythm of the beat broke, hesitated, lost revs and then came in again steadily.

There was plenty of fuel showing on the gauge.

'What's the matter with it?' she said.

'A momentary choke. Some water in the juice, perhaps.'

But she did it again, almost stopping and I nosed down towards the angry sea to keep the speed. But once more she picked up and I got some more height out of her, opening up in the hope more urge would clear the dirt, or water, or whatever it was.

'How far off are we?' she said, quickly.

'About five miles,' I said.

The smear of Gertie's arm had spread right along the port horizon now, so that it seemed to be holding Shark Island in its dreadful caress.

Suddenly Jo went to throw the wallet out of the window. I grabbed her in time and we rocked more than somewhat while I got it back.

'What's the good of it?' she panted.

'Sentimental value,' I said, and stuffed it back in my pocket.

The engine coughed again, longer this time. I put the nose down a bit and eased

74

the throttle to see if she would smooth-out at some other setting. But she started running very roughly. There was obviously trouble aboard now, and I began to regret the non-existence of Mel's inspection.

'What is it?' she said.

'Sounds like a carburettor full of Caribbean sand,' I said. 'We might make it, but it won't be happy.'

She looked out of the window and down from the rocking cabin.

'We can't swim in that sea,' she said.

'You may have to. If a shark comes up, just shout and he'll go away.'

She stared straight ahead at the island. We still had plenty of height, but the wind was turning on the compass and heading straight at us, playing its old game of gusting at sixty knots or so, reducing our effective forward speed by that amount.

The engine ran raggedly and shook in the frame. Jo looked round and up at the Piper.

'We're slowing a lot,' I said. 'Is he coming up?'

'No. He's still a long way off.'

I wiped the sweat off my face with my

arm. It was hot in that cabin. The general atmosphere of heat and dread was like standing by while a demon stoker opened an oven door.

Then just to cool it a bit, the engine picked up on all four again and we made better flying in the teeth of the battling wind.

'I don't know — ' she cried out suddenly. My heart sank.

'He's changed somehow,' she went on. 'I can't make out how.'

I looked round and up. He'd changed attitude all right. Instead of sailing slowly on up there with his nose in the air, he was pointing down, hardly visible now for the slimness of the head-on silhouette against the storm sky.

'He's coming down,' I shouted. 'Just get a grip on this and if he comes near, pot him as best you can — if you get the chance.'

I gave her my gun.

'And don't get excited,' I said. 'Don't get so keen on hitting him you shoot your pilot.'

'The damn things you joke about!' she

snapped, and I saw her thumb up the safety catch as if this was not the first time she'd done it.

Shark Island was then just over two miles away. It looked like a giant jelly studded all over with trees, with a great white house set on the southern side, looking out over the yellow day.

'Mel must have done beach landings,' I said. 'I see nowhere for a strip anywhere on top there.'

The bucketing was intense even at fifteen hundred feet. I could see a wide strip of beach on the leeward of the island. With this gusting gale coming down the forested slopes on to the beach there would be more general turbulence than it bore thinking about.

'He's gaining like mad,' she said, urgently.

'Hope he blows his tail off,' I said grimly. 'That can happen, but it needs a lot of luck.'

I looked round. She had not exaggerated. He was coming down on us like a bat out of hell, although he was still some distance off.

The only hope was to motor down on to the beach and just dig in any way that it would hurt the least. The way the Piper was coming down he didn't look as if he would try a landing — not yet, anyway.

We seemed to be just hanging in the air off the island and dancing around like a toy on a string. I started to put her down and gain some speed. I reckoned with this head wind I could lose what height I wanted when the time came and other problems had to be faced.

For a moment it seemed we held him, but it was just a difference in speeds varying, because he got bigger all the time though not as fast as before.

The engine was running better, but wasn't right; I felt that if it was pushed it would cut.

The marksman's old problem remained; he couldn't keep his aircraft level enough at any given moment to get a good shot, though he must have been a hot aimer, for in those storm conditions of bouncing he had hit us twice already.

He was about half a mile behind and coming down fast when we came nearly over the beach. My obvious move was to lose height in a big gliding full turn leaving myself heading for the beach again, low down and close to it.

With plenty of engine.

And luck. But the engine was the main thing. If that kept going we might bend the luck to our side.

'He's almost on us!' she called out.

I looked back. He was coming on to our tail and about four hundred yards off. Both planes were bumping around, rocking badly, but the rifleman had overcome that disadvantage before.

The engine came in hard as I opened the throttle and banked over into a steep turn right in front of him. What avoiding action he took I didn't see, but he overran us badly and went swooping out over the trees in a flattish, fast turn to come back on our tail again.

We went down over the forested slope of the island above the beach. It was as rough as all hell. We were hitting bumps as if we were actually hitting the trees on our way down.

Jo was rocking in the seat, and but for

the safety belt would have been hurt more than a little.

The engine was all right at this point, but my object was to make the last turn low over the sea, making allowance for the way the wind would be pushing us out during the turn, then motor in hard for the beach and pile up on the sand almost any way that didn't kill us.

As we went down the cliff I looked back and saw the Piper appear over the top, his wings rocking. We were making some unpleasant sort of ground speed over the cliffs then, with the wind behind us. It seemed to grab our tail and shake it from side to side in the effort to shove us on faster.

I told her what I meant to do in one syllable words, and only about twenty of them.

'Just sit as tight as you can, and if we hit the sea, wait till the shock goes and then pull the pin out of the belt.'

'Yes,' she said.

We tore out over the beach. I could see sand and leaves, even bits of driftwood moving, whirling and spinning in the wind as if things were trying to come up from underneath.

Before we came over the crashing sea below, I gave her the gun and banked right over to make the turn. It put our transparent roof right in the line of the oncoming Piper for, it seemed, seconds on end.

Jo fired my revolver three times while we were drifting out, bottom first over the sea and struggling, it felt, to get the nose round towards the beach again.

The engine didn't falter. Sweat ran into my eyes, but my two hands were busy with the control stick and the throttle, easing out of the turn fairly slowly in case the gusting put us near the stall point and threw us into the sea.

She came round, the engine pulling hard and I nosed her down the last fifty feet to the beach, fighting every cubic inch of air coming off the screaming island.

A couple of shots went through the port wing near me. I saw the holes come in the fabric, and, like the first, they started to strip back in the wind.

'We'll make it!' I said.

And it was then I thought the Piper pilot had gone mad.

He was flying down on to the beach, with the gusting gale right behind him, and making a flat turn towards us.

'What's he doing?'

She was pointing the revolver through the windscreen.

There wasn't time enough to answer. We seemed to be coming in over the creaming edge of the wild sea at about twenty miles an hour, rocking badly.

At this rate, if we touched down we'd be blown over backwards if a real thumper got hold of us just too soon. But as long as the engine kept churning on, I had a measure of control.

'He's going to fly into us!' she screamed out.

It looked as if he had lost control partly, for his flat turn was still going on, bringing his nose round across our path.

I dared not risk any sudden turn then. I couldn't understand why he did such a thing in those conditions.

As he turned, it seemed his tail skidded

out and round towards us, only forty feet up off the beach.

I had gone too far to change my mind about landing then. There is a point of no return for such decisions, and we were past it.

The one way left for us to get in, if only half alive and in a wreck, and that was dead ahead, as far as I could hold it ahead.

And the Piper was swinging out of control dead ahead of us.

Then suddenly I saw a whirl of oil smoke pour out of his cowling, and I saw what was amiss too clearly.

As flames burst out of the cowling, the prop jerked and practically stopped.

'You've hit his engine!' I said.

That was about all the time there was to talk.

He flicked over, one wing tip hit the sand and dug in. The Piper rolled on to its back and flame, smoke and bursting sand blotted out my landing path ahead.

We were making only about twenty miles an hour, but suddenly the wind broke. We shot forward at the full seventy-five with the engine on. I cut it, and tried to get the wheels running on the sand. But in the sudden calm she leapt up again, sailing forward like a lunatic intent on destruction.

I couldn't open up again. There was only the cliff to hit if I did that. I couldn't turn.

We just had to go on and crash into the flaming wreck.

4

To ease the speed of the accident I pushed the stick forward and got the wheels digging the sand. We see-sawed, but there was some deceleration. Then suddenly we had luck.

A terrific gust of wind came smack in our nose just when I had that nose pushed down, trying to get braking from the earth and not, as usual, the air. It shuddered us from end to end and one wing tip scraped up a flying fan of sand. A few yards from the wreck we must have been down to about twenty knots, quite suddenly and luckily. I put on left rudder and brakes.

She wheeled round, heeled under the wind, scraped up more sand with the port wing while the starboard one swept right through the flames and smoke shooting up from the Piper.

We hit something and jarred, but we were sagging then and finally came to a stop on the tailwheel, port wheel and port wing tip, held there in the flaming smoke by the tearing wind.

The gust died as suddenly as it had come, and another scurry came tearing across the beach from another direction, brushing the flames away along our starboard side. Our aircraft tottered and then lumped over on to both wheels of the undercart.

'You missed it!' she screamed in relief.

As we stopped I saw a face at the window of the blazing Piper. It was yellow brown and it was burning, but even at that distance, and in a brief glance, it seemed to me the man was dead.

Then on the other side of the wreck I saw a man running, a rifle slung across his back. He was running for the trees and the cliff.

The glimpse was momentary, for the wind eased and the blaze and smoke of the pyre rose straight up, blotting out sight of the runner.

'Get out and away from this,' I said.

In the relief and the noise of the fire I thought my motor had stopped, but then

I tried it and she answered.

'No, hang on, we can move out,' I shouted.

We taxied, bumping on the sand and swaying in the terrific gusts. We rocked hopelessly. Sooner or later the wind was going to come in the right direction and turn the plane over on to her back.

Then I saw a Land-Rover station wagon tearing across the sand towards us. I forgot all thought of enemies, agents, men with and without wallets, and gave a shout of relief.

The vehicle stopped a few yards away and a couple of blacks jumped out and ran to us. They grabbed our wing tips as if they had done this before. Then a brown man came and added his weight where it was most needed. Often one would be swung right off the sand and left dangling from the tip under a sudden gust.

But with engine, luck, some small skill and the acrobatics of the handlers we got the tattered Auster right in under the lee of a fifty-foot cliff.

The third man came to the cabin door, gesturing. I opened it and he snaked in behind me, got some screw pickets from the locker behind me and got out again and they all lashed the plane down to firm ground so that only the full force of a hurricane would move it.

We got out.

The Land-Rover, empty, stood on the sand, its rubber mudflaps blowing against the wheels by the wind scurrying on the sand.

A big, fat man was standing looking at the blazing wreck, watching the burning man inside. The fat man's trousers and jacket streamed forward of him like straining flags. His hair was unruffled. He was bald as a ball.

'Gabriel Pachmann,' Jo yelled in my ear. She held her hair from smothering her face.

The fat man turned to us, then indicated the Land-Rover. He went to it himself and got into the driver's seat. We ran up, made breathless by the wind, and got in the seat beside him.

He had a heavy face, but he did not look old. In fact, his fatness gave him a smooth, even cherubic complexion. By

88

his build and features he looked like some professional wrestler who had shaved his hair to stop his opponents getting a handful.

His eyes were narrow, pouched in the fat, and a very bright green. They swept Jo, as if there would be time to know her later, then looked at me.

Slowly his face changed, hardened, then became quizzical.

He had been expecting Mel.

'You were very foolish to fly in such weather,' he said.

He looked across the sands to the burning aircraft. Beyond it ours had been made as fast as could be until the storm came in full strength.

'It wasn't all the weather that was exciting,' I said. 'We've been having an air battle with rifles and pistols. Just like grandfather in 1914.'

He grunted and started the engine. He got a low gear to heave out of the sand. It was streaming over the beach like thin smoke now and we could see the whorls where the changes of wind made eddies.

'I thought,' he said, as we lurched

forward, 'that it was Barney's plane.'

'It is,' I said. 'We are friends of Barney's.'

Jo pressed against me but I didn't know if it was a signal for caution or not. She knew a lot about Pachmann. I knew really nothing at all.

We ran off the beach and started climbing a winding narrow road between the heavy foliage of the hillside. The car wasn't noisy and I noticed the usual screaming and screeching of birds was missing.

They go like that before the full hurricane comes. My short experience of these islands had taught me that.

'Is Gertie coming back?' I said.

'It is tracking round again,' Pachmann said. 'They say that some of its force is dying out, but there will be plenty left, I think.'

He smiled as if at some pleasant kind of joke. I felt a cringing sensation in my heart. When Gertie had gone away, she didn't seem so bad, but now she was coming back again in full force, I didn't feel so good.

'One of the men from that plane ran into the wood,' Jo said.

Gabriel nodded.

'He will be caught,' he said. 'There is no one on this island but my friends, my servants and me.'

It seemed to trap the fellow just with words, it was so easy.

'Tell me who they were,' he went on. 'The numbers were all burnt off.'

'We didn't actually read any numbers,' I said. 'Conditions were not ideal.'

We joined another road, still under heavy trees, and then broke out on to a terrace before the house. There were two or three black servants taking in garden furniture and closing and locking shutters over the windows.

'Battening down the hatches before the storm,' Gabriel said, and laughed so that his fat cheeks shook. 'But we are well protected here. You should be very comfortable.'

We got out by the veranda steps, mounted them and went into the house. It was some house. If Gabriel lived by buying and selling international secrets, then he had a formidable industry, to judge by the appearance of his domain.

In the hall, not a lot smaller than a theatre vestibule, Gabriel stopped and turned to Jo.

'You will like a bath,' he said and snapped his fingers. 'This is Sarah — ' Sarah had come from nowhere, silent, black and smiling a melon slice of teeth, ' — and she will look after you.'

Jo glanced at me, and for the first time in an hour or so, I looked at her critically. She was certainly in a mess. The bumpy flight had done no good to her dress, in fact it had ripped the zipper out at the back, and the rest of her had gathered a good deal of sand and sooty smut from the fire.

And yet, like that, I thought her more attractive than well groomed.

She went off with the woman servant, and Gabriel led me into a luxurious study. It could have been in England, but there were too many West Indian touches.

He gave me a Scotch, as if he quite understood how I felt. He did not spoil it with lumps of ice, as if he knew I hate diluting booze.

'Now Mr. — ?' he said.

'Jonathan Blake,' I said.

'Well, Jonathan, I am Gabriel Pachmann, but we don't use surnames on this island. It is not often a great help afterwards. Some visitors have more than one, others change with the whim of the moment.'

He shook with laughter and his green eyes were watchful and yet laughing, too. I rather liked him. If he was a rogue he was a genial one, and I have always had the sneak liking for a villain. Heroes are so pale.

Then he held out his hand for a moment.

'You have a message for me?' he said.

The wallet was in my pocket, and while only Jo and I knew it had nothing in it, it could have some value. Once anybody else knew that, it would have none.

'No,' I said, taking one of his cigarettes from a desk box. 'We were on a pleasure flip. Tried to get down on a strip at Flamingo Bay, and then this armed party flew up on us and we just bunked.

Couldn't go back because of Gertie and this island was our only hope.'

He laughed and took his hand away.

'Ah! So you are, we might say, bona fide desperadoes!'

'We were pretty desperate. In fact, we shot that plane down. Not viciously, but because we had got tired of being fired at.'

'A most reasonable attitude,' he said. 'And tell me, how is Mel? He runs the air service here for me, you know. People, goods, news — ' He stopped there.

I took a plunge which it seemed might pay back in letting me know where I'd stand, if anything got very tight in the way of suspicion.

'He isn't well,' I said.

He went sharp.

'No? How?'

'He's dead worried about something. I've known him for years and never seen anything shake him before.'

Gabriel took a cigarette.

'What do you think would worry him?' he said, and turned and watched me.

'I don't know,' I said. 'He suffered

94

damage with the hurricane, but he's insured.'

'I am surprised there was a plane left,' Gabriel said.

'A matter of luck,' I said. 'One out of six.'

One of the men who had picketed the plane came into the room. He was short, very quick and alert. He was dark, smooth haired and very thick eyebrowed. I would have put him as a Filipino; certainly not of African descent.

'This is Jim, my head man,' Gabriel said, pointing at him with his cigarette. 'Very able mechanic. Fixes cars, boats, planes, electrics, reputations — everything that ticks.'

'It is burning through,' Jim said. 'Very little to go when I left.'

'Who was the pilot?'

'Burnt up like a cork,' Jim said, and shrugged. 'But a hole in his head, and this I got.'

He held up a wrist watch and bracelet. The bracelet had been snipped in two, very roughly.

'Wire cutters,' Jim said, in explanation.

Gabriel took the watch. It was smeared with grease that had charred on it like tar.

'Did you see anything of the passenger?' Gabriel asked.

'Nothing yet. I have everybody out, but they must come in soon. The wind is back. It will be very high soon.'

Gabriel looked at the watch, back and front. Then he handed it to me.

It was a good watch. A very good watch. About a hundred and twenty pounds' worth of watch and bracelet, if I remembered my glossy adverts properly.

I turned it over. There was some engraving on the back, hard to read because of the burn smears and a slight tendency the gold had had to melt.

I rubbed it with my thumb and read.

'Pat: Good luck, sport: Mel.'

There was a date that had mostly melted off, but that didn't matter.

I looked up at Gabriel. He was looking at me thoughtfully.

'I never came across that name anywhere else,' he said almost amusingly. 'Short for Melbourne.'

'Yes,' I said. 'So he told me once.'

I couldn't believe Mel had double-crossed me, because I didn't believe he was that type.

But only he had known we would go to the strip at Flamingo Bay.

Only he had given me an empty wallet, believing I wouldn't look in it.

He had not hesitated about letting me have his one remaining aircraft.

Could Jo be right?

Was I the decoy? Or was Mel my intended vicarious murderer?

Had Pat's money persuaded him? Was his conscience the reason for his worry?

★   ★   ★

Gabriel chose that time of my doubt to think I'd like a bath. Jim took me upstairs and gave me a bedroom that might have pleased Queen Victoria. It had a bathroom which would have done the same, except for a non-plush seat.

Jim might have been a good fitter, but also was a first rate manservant. He did everything smoothly, pleasantly, as if he had been at the game all his life.

'I'd place you as being from the Philippines or thereabouts,' I said, as he unlaced my shoes.

He looked up and smiled.

'You are very close indeed,' he said.

'How come you're in the wrong ocean?'

'Big change makes big change,' he said. 'There is a lot of money around these islands. There are all sorts of trades we do not have back home.' He shrugged and looked at the ceiling as if trying to think of a sample. 'Gun-running.'

'But you've given that up?'

'For the time, yes. There are no good revolutions just now. I always get the tip-off when one is getting ready. It is a good business. I have made as much as a quarter million dollars and never smelt gun oil. It's a question of knowing the right people. But there — ' he shrugged again, ' — if you know such people, you make the money from them, then you gamble with them, and in the end they have all the big change. But then, I only go into business to make money to gamble.'

'Do you know Pat Mancini?'

'He's a cheapie.' He got up and made a contemptuous gesture.

'He wants to kill me.'

He looked sharply at me then.

'Then you should watch out. He won't do any killing but he gets guys who do. They have fancy ways, some of them. They put an explosive in a man's electric razor. I saw that one. Blew half his head off. It works when you press the comb to the face.'

'I'll grow a beard,' I said. 'The only thing is, I've got his wife. She doesn't shave.'

'The woman — Mancini's wife?' He looked very interested. 'Why then, you have a very good hold on the bastard!'

'Except that he says he'll kill her as well.'

'But he won't do that.'

I got my shirt off and went towards the bathroom, but stopped there.

'Why not?'

'Because the money is in her name,' Jim said, and now his face had the blank look of an Oriental, as if he were amused and didn't want to show it. 'You will see very soon the British Government will be after him for tax evasion. It is one of the classic fixes, but this time he has it tied so that the money is hers for sure. The lawyers won't shake it.'

Now Gabriel dealt in secrets, and with secrets come a lot of dirt. Jim could be in a very good position to know this about Mancini.

'Are you sure the money's there?' I said. 'You know, in a lot of these rich exterior cases there isn't anything inside at all. It's juggling.'

He nodded thoughtfully.

'We get good information,' he said, watching me. 'I could prove it to you. Very interesting proof, maybe.'

'All right.' I got a cigarette. They were everywhere in the house that anyone might pause for a moment. 'Be interesting.'

'You have inherited the estate of a cousin,' he said.

I didn't light the cigarette.

'I didn't hear it until four hours back.'

'We heard at the same time. We have a monitoring station on the island. Taps the phones. Very interesting tips for investment and such.'

'And how do you know this information is good?'

'At dinner Gabriel will show you the list of the investments and property in your cousin's estate,' said Jim.

'How the hell! He didn't know who I was until an hour ago!'

The mystery made me angry. It made me small. As if I were some child being smirked over by knowing adults.

'You say your name, Jonathan Blake. That goes down to the file room, and they have the phone tape from this morning — there were only a few today — and it is all tied up for reference.'

He smiled, but just managed to stop himself laughing at me.

I went and got into the bath. I sat in it, very thoughtful, but it was an uneasy kind of thought. It got uneasier still when the shutters began to drum and shudder.

Gertie was back in full dress.

When I got back in the bedroom wearing a Ghandi towel, Jim had laid an evening suit out on the bed, shirt, tie, trousers, socks, white jacket and a blood-red carnation in a small vase on the table.

What made me angrier was that everything fitted, as if he could even measure me with his smirking eyes. But perhaps they had a lot of visitors six feet two high and forty-six inch chest. Perhaps they kept clothes for all occasions down in the file room.

Down in the study again, Gabriel had changed into evening kit.

'Usually we drink on the veranda before dinner,' he said. 'But as you can hear, it is a little rumbustious right now.'

'Where's Jo?'

'Jo? Ah, Jo! She will be down, no doubt. I think you tired her with your aerobatics. That was a wonderful piece of landing. Mel would do no better. Certainly not these days. He is often drunk.'

That shook me, because Mel had been drunk that morning, and I've never known him to drink on the job, let alone be drunk. Mel was the type to have a bender on his night off and then go cold sober for the rest of the week, or month, whichever suited.

'Did you expect me? You were very quick down there.'

'We have our little radar, you know,' Gabriel said, gesturing so that a couple of big stone rings flashed in the light. 'In fact, one visitor was so kind as to call this Radio Island. We have some very fine equipment. It provides a kind of entertainment, you know, in such an isolated place.'

He looked at me with sly amusement.

'We even eavesdrop on military satellites,' he went on. 'That is quite the most entertaining of all.'

I wanted to ask him about my inheritance, but something held me back. Perhaps the small feeling I had of him knowing more about me than I did.

I also felt very uneasy about the ease and openness with which both Gabriel and Jim had told me about themselves.

If they were real spies, they certainly didn't feel they should hide anything.

And not hiding anything from me, an extremely casual dropper-in, seemed to indicate that there was nothing I could do about it even if I knew everything.

We had sherry, an Amontillado of considerable cost, but he put a twist of orange peel in his, and looking at it spoilt mine. I couldn't taste the damn stuff for orange.

'You are on holiday, Jonathan?'

'I have been. Now I must go home — when this joyful blow is over.'

'Are you thinking, perhaps of going into business in any way?'

'I have a small practice in London.'

'Oh, yes, yes, I know,' he said snapping his fingers in dismissal. 'But you surely won't think of continuing with that in the present circumstances?'

'I did hear a rumour that you were a sort of super-spy,' I said.

He laughed and drank some of his sherry.

'But I can't see why super-spies should be interested in small fry, like me.'

'My dear Jonathan, there are no small fry. All men are roughly the same size, as perhaps you have noticed. Some are more able than others, but all have a purpose, which has merely to be pointed out to them.'

'That is a wonderful and benevolent theory,' I said. 'But just too general for me.'

'Then, shall we say, every man can be a

specialist if he is lucky enough to meet the right circumstances. After all, you are a professional man. That is one side. The other is that you are an adventurer, but you don't allow the two to mix. In my view, that is an error. Professionalism and adventuring should go together as ideal partners.'

He laughed and I couldn't help doing the same, because we both knew the truth of it, and it was a truth I had always been afraid of.

What he was insinuating was that I need not now be afraid of anything. There was going to be an offer.

'Jim told me you have been looking me up,' I said. 'I must say you are very thorough. What amazes me is how quickly you can do it at the distance.'

'The first identity is fed into a computer,' he said with pleasant frankness. 'Then the requirements of the computer are flashed to the area informer where the identity is best known.

'The computer,' he went on, walking about and gesturing with his glass, 'is ideally suited to deal with character, because contrary to popular belief, it neither multiplies nor divides, but only adds and subtracts. Just, in fact, like the composition of the human character.'

I was becoming fascinated by the comprehensiveness and the ease of it all.

'Tell me what you know,' I said.

He told me about my practice, that I had been concerned with some work for the police, though not legally on their side, that I was not married, that now my cousin was dead I had no relatives.

So on his lists I could guess at a police informer in the Metropolitan area of London, and someone in my solicitors' office. That would be enough to cover everything.

The incredible fact was that they had found two such narks out of fifty million.

The thing that didn't strike me then was that they could not have found this out at that time. They must have had some reason and a line on to me *before* I'd got to this island.

But nobody had made me come here. I had been driven by my own fears, and nothing else.

'You'd like to see the content of the inheritance?' he said and pressed a bell. 'Your lawyers were most genial. We had a micro picture flashed out. We are at present using a Russian test satellite for the reflections. Most useful and economical. If only the military authorities knew the generous provision they are making for ordinary folk to prosper at no cost, or very little.'

The colossal assurance, the wicked, sophisticated humour of the man was most appealing. Though I knew it was also as dangerous as the wrong end of a loaded gun, yet it fascinated.

In a while Jim came in with a photostat of a typed list of my property. It was the summary and referred to further sheets for details.

'We just have the top sheet,' Gabriel apologised.

I was so eager to read it I didn't consider for a moment the psychological fear of Gabriel's omnipotence which was being built up in me. That list was the perfect instrument, the right anaesthetic for the job of knocking me flat later.

The rough estimate of the estate at present was 178,000 pounds, though this was based on the purchase price of property and stocks bought years before.

'You are comparatively comfortable,' Gabriel observed.

'I never knew I had such wise kin.'

Again he laughed, but I could not see anything so funny about it. The time was getting on, the storm was rising. There were a lot of small, half muffled sounds from outside such as I had heard — and been frightened to death of — before. The slapping of a door, a dustbin bowling along, tiles falling and smashing, unnamed objects being grunched along on rough ground, people shouting warnings, half lost in the wind bellow. It was the whole atmosphere of real disaster come all over again.

And it all reminded me of Jo.

I had not seen her since we had arrived, and I had a queer feeling — perhaps brought on by fear of the storm and unnamed apprehension of Gabriel's ideas — that she was in some danger.

He walked around, talking of international

things, of shipping disguises and organised revolutions. While he did it I tried to sort out my feelings.

The news of the details of my fortune had struck numbly. It just was too far away to mean much. It promised a wild difference in my life — but in a far distant place. At present I was stranded on a sunburnt, storm-swept island, and I had the odd sensation that it wouldn't be all that easy to get off again.

Jim came in.

'Dinner's ready, Gabriel,' he said.

It was ridiculous. He hadn't learnt the part this time. I remember playing the butler in some play and being brayed at by the woman producer, 'Lunch is ready: dinner is served!' But everytime she shouted it at me she got it wrong and in the end there was chaos.

'But where is the lady?' I asked.

Gabriel looked enquiringly at Jim. It was a very brief look but I caught it while draining my glass.

'She pleads a headache,' Jim said, his quiet, broad smile across his face. 'She may come down later.'

★ ★ ★

We dined just the two of us, with Jim hovering. He was certainly a gem in a place like this. He was as good a butler as a valet, but he was too catlike, too quiet. I kept thinking he would slip up and whisper over my shoulder, 'Want to buy a gun?'

We talked of many things, general things, nothing pointed at all. I began to get impatient for him to get at what was in his mind.

Then when we were eating fruit, Jim left us.

'I want your partnership in a venture,' Gabriel said, his eyes steadily fixed on mine.

'I've no mind to go into business. Investments — '

'I don't want your money,' he said. 'We are not hard up for dross. What I am in need of is hardness, know-how and experience of certain avenues of stealth.'

'I have none of those values.'

'It's my opinion that matters. You will come in with us.'

'No.' I was dead against him then. I thought he was going to play Jo as the damsel in distress.

'But yes,' he said. 'You are a young man and can look forward to a rich life when the excitement is over. After all, no one wants the excitement to go on and spoil comfort in the end.'

He stuffed a handful of grapes into his mouth and chewed a while. I just shook my head. It wasn't much point in going on saying No.

'You have a double,' he said. 'Right nearby. You have heard of him?'

'Yes.'

'You must be careful. Suitably briefed, he could go back to England instead of you and take the money.'

Then he laughed, and so did I. I hadn't been able to see why anybody should want to have my double. Now I did.

5

Gabriel kept on eating grapes, stuffing in handfuls as if he might be blown up before he finished them. The wind was thundering around the house then, and small ornaments and fitments were starting to move.

'At present it is no use offering you money,' Gabriel said, his mouth still half full. 'But later, perhaps, when money makes you greedy again. That will take some time, however, we wish for now.'

This indicated that the idea of a double gathering up the goods instead of me was not his entirely, and therefore he was willing to shelve it in favour of the more direct line.

'Just tell me more about this double,' I said. 'It interests me.'

'A coincidence,' he said, shrugging. 'You come on holiday. There is somebody like you. Seen together no one would be fooled, but apart, yes. He has been trained in your mannerisms. That is what counts, of course.'

'And how have I been watched that well?'

'Bugged with cameras,' said Gabriel and laughed. 'They can afford anything in the Caribbean.'

'They must have been very interested in me,' I said.

'I think first it was meant to be blackmail on the woman,' he said, using a toothpick and sucking the result. 'Then, when the news came of your good fortune, it switched, you see.'

'Who could be so interested?'

'Many people about these islands live by being interested in others. It's a major industry.'

'What is it you need help about?'

He laughed and watched me with narrow, fat-pouched eyes.

'I have a spy here,' he said.

'Funny. I thought you were a spy.'

'I am an information exchange centre. If the Russians invaded me, the British would come and throw them out, and if the Chinese came, the Americans would throw *them* out, and all vice versa and about turn as you say. We are, like the great whore, hated but required by all and sundry. It is a staggeringly profitable business. I expect one day to be knighted, awarded the Legion d'Honneur, made a freeman of Washington — But you understand?'

'What I don't understand is this spy.'

'He is selling information before I can,' said Gabriel, offering a cigar box. 'He is one of my men here, but I can't tell which, and if I look, he will know I am looking.

'But he also knows that you landed here in a bad emergency. He probably knows by now you would be valuable to me because of your good fortune. He will think at once that I will be leading you up the garden path. He will consider you the absolute outsider.

'With your experience you would be able to sniff him out and shoot him.'

I laughed then. It was the airy, casual way he said these outrageous things that made it all seem ridiculous.

Except that I knew, with a cold

realisation, that he meant it. On his island he probably did shoot people if he felt like it. He didn't seem to be under any kind of outside jurisdiction. In fact, as he had said, nations doing business with him would ensure nothing interfered with his well-being.

He was cunning old Fury, Judge, Jury and Executioner.

It gave me a long cold look at my own position there. I could also be shot, and nobody would do anything about it. In fact, I wouldn't die having the pleasure of knowing somebody would pay for it.

Rather somebody I didn't know would step into my shoes in England.

I didn't like that either. I never thought I should be so fussy about things that would happen after I was shot dead.

It must have been Gabriel's wine.

He was watching me and smoking his cigar slowly.

'How many people have you got here?'

'Fifty-three.'

'That's a lot.'

'Twenty-one women and girls, twenty men, all coloured; eleven Europeans

— on radio work, and Jim.'

'How are the Europeans split up?'

'Three engineers, eight radio operators. We always have two on watch, four in busy times. Now, you think about it. I have a call to make, long distance.'

He went to the door when I called him.

'Do you have any caller using a Piper Cub aircraft?' I said.

He looked at his cigar.

'I have had one or two such. Hire jobs from the eastern end of the island.' He shrugged. 'Always different people. A lot of the people I do business with don't leave much in the way of identity. Aircraft round about are no stranger than cabs. It's as cheap as a boat — if you can fly.'

He went out.

The way he'd presented it, it was as if this was something he had just thought of, something that had occurred after we had crash-landed on the beach.

But to me it didn't seem like that. It seemed to have begun a long time before tonight.

Looking back, the thread ran from the

original fear of Mancini's hired killers, to the airfield which could have been foreseen, as Mel was an old friend and I had hired planes from him in the last few days before Gertie turned up.

Mel's direction had been to land on the strip at Flamingo Bay, but the Piper had been waiting for us.

And honestly speaking, it had driven us out to sea, if only by the manoeuvre of keeping between us and the land.

We had arrived over Shark Island together, and Gabriel and his men had been waiting.

Then came the shock.

Jo had fired out with my revolver in conditions of the roughest. She had fired three shots, I think, and of those one had caught fire to his engine and the other had gone through the pilot's head.

Which was the biggest incredible factor of the whole weird routine.

I am a practised revolver shot. I shoot competitions. I am a champion in my own small world. For this high standard of shoot I use Smith and Wesson twenty-two automatics of long barrel design with every means provided for accurate shooting. It means an accuracy near to a rifle, but it also means it isn't handy. You can't slip it in your pocket.

My thirty-eight is a compromise between accuracy and portability. It's accurate up to a point, but as more yards come between it and the target, so the directness becomes vague.

I couldn't have hit that aircraft from the Auster in those circumstances. There was extreme bumpiness, the calculation of angle and interception speeds, a tearing gusting wind to affect the bullet, and finally the distance range.

In the excitement and relief of finding we had got away with our necks, I hadn't thought of these things before.

Now that I did I saw that the likeliest explanation of the Piper's end was that it had been shot by rifle fire from the ground.

Such a shot wouldn't be easy, but it would be ten times simpler and more certain than Jo's blasting out of the Auster window.

So if, as it seemed likely, the Piper had

been shot by someone on Shark Island then it was most likely done by Gabriel.

He had watched the burn-up, not us. It hadn't been till he'd turned that he'd seen I wasn't Mel.

Then he had been surprised.

That switched the whole thing back to the start because it meant he hadn't known it was me in the Auster, and therefore my earlier connections didn't count.

He came back and closed the door carefully behind him.

'Have you thought?' he said.

'Yes. I'll do it — but on one condition.'

He cocked his head.

'Condition?' he said suspiciously.

'You let Jo out.'

He really laughed then. He threw his head back, lost the carefully kept ash from his cigar, and his fat body shook until his loose, thin suit bellied and trembled like a sail in an uncertain breeze.

'What made you think I kept her prisoner?' he said, wiping his eyes.

'Just a thought.'

He pointed at me with the cigar like my schoolmaster used to with his threatening bit of chalk.

'And,' he said, 'you are right!' He smoked again and rang the bell for Jim. 'But you show too, that I am right. You know what to expect of people. That is very valuable training. Trust is the most dangerous of traitors.'

Jim came in.

'We would like to see Mrs. Mancini,' said Gabriel.

Jim just bowed his head and went out again.

'You must have some idea of the man you want,' I said.

'I narrow to four,' he said. 'But I could be wrong about that. Let me enumerate:

'Chang Lee, Chinese from Hong Kong. British passport. On radio watch.

'Gaston Domenic, Italian from Malta, British passport. Also radio watch.

'John Addison, Plymouth, served as radio operator, British Navy, engineer.

'Willi Heinz, German from Hanover, radio watch and second engineer.'

He watched me again.

'Three of these men cover the language difficulty, it seems.'

'Lee speaks Chinese, Japanese, Malay and some Russian. Very gifted. Domenic, Italian, French, Greek, Hebrew, Arabic. Addison speaks Hindustani. Heinz speaks Swedish, Polish, Czech, Hungarian. Very useful men.'

'Key men.'

'The other operators on watch are all at least bilingual, some multi. Our business is international, you understand. Nothing must be lost for lack of an unknown word.'

'Three out of four have British passports.'

He shrugged.

'Surely nothing extraordinary?' he said. 'The sun may have set on the Empire but not quite yet on its passports.'

'Everything coming in is taped?'

'Indeed. And everything going out.' He looked cunning then. 'Nobody can send any private message without the other man on watch knowing.'

'Then how does your spy send his information out?'

Gabriel gestured with a big, fat hand glowing with rings.

'Air. Boat.'

The thundering of the wind on the house was not so great as it had been, or perhaps I was getting used to it.

'What kind of information has been going out?'

I had the idea he wouldn't answer that, and I was right. He walked away, talking about these four men, telling me little things about them he thought I should know.

'But I think it is only one,' he said, stopping and turning to me. 'It is most important to find him!'

He rattled the last words out with a suddenness that showed for the first time, a nervous Caesar. Previously secure in his hideout he was suddenly on the lookout for daggers.

It must have been an extraordinary coincidence that I crashed on the island only that afternoon. I couldn't stomach that. It was just too extraordinary.

'Is there a lot of armament around?'

He looked at me quickly.

'Some automatic rifles, pistols, hunting weapons.'

'Quite an arsenal. Where are they?'

'Locked in the room next to this,' he said, pointing at a wall.

'The key?'

He pulled a golden chain from his pocket and swung some keys on the end of it.

'No others?'

'Not for important places like that.' He grinned.

The door opened, Jim grinned at it. Jo came through, tall, haughty, very beautiful and in a magnificent rage. Jim bowed mockingly at her back and withdrew.

'Thank the Lord you're all right!' Jo said, stopping in front of me.

I could see in her face she really did care. It made me embarrassed, pleased and helpless.

'I've been all right all the time,' I said. 'I'm sorry you missed dinner. There aren't even any grapes left.'

'They brought me food,' she said. 'I left it. That Japanese grins like a monkey.'

'He's more Polynese,' I said.

'Why did you lock me up?' she said, turning on Gabriel.

'He said it would be safer,' Gabriel said, and flicked his cigar towards me.

She turned back to me in genuine amazement.

'Leave it,' I said. 'You can't win when it comes to the truth. Just agree.'

'Is that what you've done?'

Her look was penetrating. I wondered how she knew.

★ ★ ★

Gabriel went to the door.

'I'll leave you to chat it over. I have some things to attend to,' he said, and went out.

'What do you know?' I said. 'And if so, who told you?'

'The Polynesian totem pole,' she said angrily. 'If you ask me, the place is fuller of bugs than a Polynesian mattress.'

'But they only locked you in, didn't they?' I asked, specially cool.

'Only? I'm damn not used to being locked in anywhere by anybody! I'm not — '

'I agreed to work with them to let you out,' I said. 'What's the fury? I should get thanks not rockets.'

I got hold of her arm and squeezed it hard till it hurt and she held herself back a little. Then I told her what I'd agreed to do.

'But why?' she said.

'Because we'll never get off the island otherwise. Gabriel makes it look like an offer but it's a kind of mantrap. So it would be well to discuss the matter calmly.'

She walked away, not liking to give way.

'The storm's dying,' she said, cocking her head at the ceiling.

'So it should. It's been overdoing it,' I said.

All the same, the idea of getting out of being shut in that place was demanding. We went out into the hall and on to the veranda.

The hurricane had gone by. There was still a stiff wind lashing the thick tree tops, but the night was clear and a bright moon lit everything with a kindly silver glow. It showed a lot of wreckage about, bits of wood, tiles, trees, rubbish blown by from somewhere behind the yard walls.

There were three coloured men clearing up, loading long iron wheelbarrows with the stuff. One chanted some kind of calypso made up about his mother-in-law who had a nose like a pear.

We walked by, and their eye whites flashed, watching us. There were teeth, too, but they came later, when they guessed who we were.

Round on the terrace looking down on the sea there was a strong, hot wind, which seemed to warn Gertie hadn't quite cleared the area. The big paper flowers in the bushes on the slope whipped and ducked furiously.

It was the sort of wind to carry voices away.

I told her everything Gabriel had said to me, and she listened impatiently.

'I still think you're a fool, getting involved with him,' she said afterwards. 'You know what he is! If you go in with him on anything you'll be stuck for good. You'll never get free of him! Don't say you will because I know!'

'We get on well,' I said. 'You worry too much.'

'But why do it?'

'There is a mild compulsion,' I said. 'But on top, it's something to do and I'm mad keen to know why these characters have picked on me.'

'Pat!' she fairly exploded. 'That's who it is. My dear husband!'

'Do you really think Gabriel would mess around with one small petty jealousy fit-up?'

Yet all the same, when she said it, the connection seemed to ring bells. I suppose because it went back to what I had been thinking, of someone driving us out here.

But if it had started with Pat, I was sure the motive wasn't jealousy. It would have to be a good deal more than that to get Gabriel interested.

'What does Pat do these days — apart from gambling?' I said.

'They have a syndicate. Playing the markets.'

'He gambles a lot?'

'Men do when the luck turns against them.'

'It's turned against him?'

'He gets bad patches.' She wasn't inclined to talk about him. 'Have you thought what we're going to do?'

'You mean about Pat? No.'

It struck me then I'd been deliberately trying not to think of what to do. Even this tie-up with Gabriel was all part of a delaying tactic subconsciously aimed at putting off what I was going to do about Jo.

'What do you want to do?' I asked.

'The weather's getting better. We could go in the morning if it holds.'

'Go where?'

'Well — get away from here! We're worse off here than we were.'

I spotted someone moving amongst the trees to the left of her shoulder.

'Go on putting your case,' I said softly. 'We're being shadowed.'

She was good. She went on talking, angrily, but mostly repeating what she had said already in different forms. But as that's what women usually do when they're riled it must have sounded the right stuff.

Anyway, the watcher backed away in the trees and turned to go.

'Hang on here,' I said, and vaulted the low stone wall of the terrace.

The ground was soft and I learnt long ago to keep quiet if someone is likely to be listening. The man ahead was ambling along lazily, his hips swaying. In fact, his left hip was very prominent.

I felt certain he had a gun there.

Unless Gabriel had told me a lot of lies, there shouldn't have been any guns on the island outside his arsenal room.

Except, of course, the rifle the Piper man had landed with.

Then I remembered that the running figure I had seen so briefly through the blowing smoke and flame had been wearing a khaki sort of shirt. This man wore white, which was why I had seen him so easily.

As I followed him he had a kind of insolent swagger which put the smell of warning in my nostrils.

I came close up behind him. He knew,

for I could see the slight contraction of his muscles as he moved, abandoning the swagger.

Then he swung round.

The moonlight shafted down through the trees there, and in its light the broad blade of a knife flashed. It could have been a machete, but to my English eye it looked as big as a broad-bladed billhook.

Luckily, I'd expected a movement and ducking, got him low down. I threw him over my head and he went down heavily, but rolled over like an acrobat and was crouching on his feet again almost instantly.

But without the knife.

He came at me and I recognised judo. Luckily, again, I know judo. I'm no good at it but it's a big advantage to know it because you have an idea what he is going to do.

The result was he didn't get my assistance when he gripped me. Instead I went flaccid and he was left trying to hump a fourteen stone pudding for a split second.

I was just right in position for a short

arm clunk under his jaw, and got a lot of strength behind it. In the moonlight it looked as if I had knocked his head off.

He went backwards and fell on his knees, but he was not knocked that silly, for his hand came on the fallen knife and he grabbed it up and raised it.

This time I kicked him in the face, and he went over backwards. Then I jumped on him and spasmodically, he let the knife go, tried to grip it again, then let it go.

I got him by his collar and hauled him up with his back against a tree. He grunted, at which I wasn't surprised and took some time getting his breath back.

Meanwhile I got the gun out of his pocket. I was puzzled as to why he hadn't used it until I snapped out the magazine.

It was empty. Perhaps Gabriel issued empty guns. They could be of great use in certain circumstances.

The man was Chinese, judging from his face.

'You shouldn't have done that to a stranger,' I said.

He just looked at me, and then his eyes narrowed right down.

'Is your name *Lee*?' I asked him.

He stared for a minute, then shook his head.

'Not Lee, no. Simpson.'

Anybody can call themselves what they like, and I could be Who Wang Ho, if I felt like it, but this was the most unlikely Simpson I had ever seen.

But if this wasn't Lee, then according to Gabriel's list of his employees, Simpson didn't fit anywhere.

'Why were you watching me?' I asked him.

'Not you. The woman.'

'Why the woman?'

He hesitated a moment, then he felt his face tenderly.

'I am paid to find the woman.'

'Who pays you?'

He shrugged.

'I don't know. Nobody ever knows. Comes the middleman with the money. That's all.'

'And who's the middleman, then?'

'No name,' he said, shaking his head, but he described the German I had seen in the hotel that morning, the one Jo had said was called Muck.

'Where do you see this man?'

'Flamingo Bay.'

'How did you get here?'

He grinned, then held his arm out and pointed.

'The needle,' he said.

True or not, it was a splendid way to get out of answering questions.

'You just woke up here?'

'Just woke up. Yes.'

'How did you know the woman?'

'I have picture.'

I held out my hand. He rummaged in his shirt and I watched carefully for what he brought out, just in case.

It was a photograph of a magnificently built woman with a strangely fascinating, ugly face. Certainly it wasn't Jo.

'This isn't the woman,' I said.

'Yes. That woman,' he said, and pointed back towards the terrace.

'You couldn't have seen her face.'

'Yes. I see her face.' He pointed to the photo. 'That one. I see.'

Jo had had her back to him when I'd spotted him.

'Did you see us come on to the terrace?'

'Yes. I see. You and the woman. This woman. Yes.'

He tapped the photo with his finger.

There was little point in arguing with him because he was obviously convinced he hadn't made a mistake.

Something made me uneasy about that mis-identification, but I didn't know what then. A lot of other thoughts were buzzing in my head.

'We might do business,' I said. 'You work for money. I give money for work.'

'Yes?' he said, and seemed quite eager.

'How are you going to get off the island?' I asked.

'I get signal. They will come.'

'Suppose they don't?'

He sat against the tree and thought and said nothing.

'They come,' he said at last. 'Because they must know for certain.'

'What must you do for them?'

'To kill the woman.'

I felt the old cold grab at my heart, fear of something I really knew already.

'What about me?'

'You?' He stared. 'Not you. No, not you.'

'You had a good try just now.'

'Self defence,' he said, and grinned again. 'Anybody kill anybody on this island. 'Tis all right. Okay. Nobody care.'

'You know the island?'

'I have been before.'

In view of Gabriel's radar protection belt and similar devices, I wondered how this was being done. But the needle prevented me from knowing.

'You get the needle going back?'

He nodded. I looked at his arm again.

'You're rather fond of the needle, aren't you?'

'Very pleasant.'

'You get the signal when they will come?'

'Okay. Yes.'

'You must have somewhere here that you hide?'

He hesitated now, and for a while refused to speak. I tossed up whether to bash him into talking or give him cash. In the end I got my wallet and started counting money.

'There is a place. Yes.'

'You'll show me?'

Now he looked up and for the first time stared into my eyes.

'If you tell, you die,' he said, very simply.

'Yes.'

He reached out to grab the money, but I pulled back and only gave him two of the notes. He shrugged and took them, stuffing them in his shirt together with the woman's photograph.

'I show,' he said, and got up.

He would have bent and got his knife back, but I trod on it and waited for him to go by. Again he shrugged and went on. He was very philosophical. I wondered how he had started in the murder business. But then you can never tell what some people will enjoy.

We went down a winding path hedged in with high ferns.

The wind had died a lot by then, and the air was fresh and cool.

We didn't go far down the path before he dodged to one side and vanished behind a mass of fern. I darted up smartly, but when I got there, he was crouching down by a huge stone, waiting for me.

He nodded when he saw me.

The stone was set in the steep slope up which the path ran. He pushed it on the right corner and the whole massive piece revolved inward, leaving a black space to one side, about a foot wide and four high.

He nodded to me, as if for my approval.

I squatted down beside him.

'What you say about dying applies to you, too. You understand?'

'You kill me?' he said, sharp and suspicious again.

'Yes. If you tell anyone I know.'

Then I got him by the throat and hung on, almost cracking his windpipe. He didn't struggle much. I let him go and he fell against the stone, gasping.

'You see?' I said.

He nodded.

I was satisfied he would be a useful ally now he'd been inoculated with both fear and money. I went slowly up the path.

Some way up I stopped where there was a break in the trees and looked down towards the beach on which we had landed only a few hours before.

The sea sparkled like sequins, flashing the moon. Where it broke down on the sands the line was phosphorescent, a green silver line.

But the beach was empty. There was no sign of the Piper wreck there now.

I went on back to the terrace. She was waiting there in her white dress — no doubt supplied from one of Gabriel's extensive guest wardrobes — leaning against the terrace wall. She was smoking, her back to me.

I came on to the terrace and she turned to me.

'You've been ages, Johnny,' she said.

She looked at me, and I looked at her.

It wasn't Jo. It was the splendid ugly woman in Simpson's picture.

6

Some shocks come so heavily that they don't seem to have an impact. They just go right through your sensitivity and leave you much as you were before, but with a problem.

The woman was smiling at me. She had stepped into Jo's part, slipped in, taken over, gone on where I had left Jo off, standing on the terrace, waiting for me.

'Where have you been, darling?'

'I went to see a man,' I said.

She was playing in Jo's wicket, and it didn't look to me as if asking for explanations was going to help.

Quite suddenly I decided to reverse the score and play along as if she was Jo. That would, I thought, push her back a lot, because instead of making me wonder what was the matter with me, she was going to begin to wonder what had happened to her.

'What man?' she said, taking my arm.

'A yellow man with red hair. He was carrying a picture of you.'

She laughed. She had a good, easy way with her, graceful so that the ugliness of her large, loose mouth, the thick brows and the too-high cheekbones didn't matter. They were animated into something, not ugly, but vivacious and magnetic.

'Have you thought this out?' she asked, watching me.

'What?' I thought that would give her the ball back and leave her where she had started.

'Whether you'll help Gabriel or not.'

The ball was back in my hands so that it stung. She could have been the Jo I had been talking to, only she wasn't.

'I haven't made up my mind,' I said.

She was another thing I couldn't make up my mind about. She had stepped into Jo's place apparently knowing what Jo had talked about.

According to Gabriel, there was no white woman on the island but Jo. Gabriel was not necessarily to be trusted, but secure in his own fortress, why should he want to lie?

Or didn't he know?

The objection to his not knowing about an interminable queue of travellers coming to his island unsuspected was that undoubtedly, Gabriel had the place watched very carefully.

Simpson had got here and nobody knew how, including Simpson. They just blotted his head out and he came to again, finding himself on Shark Island.

Perhaps other people could be shipped in that way, too, but it didn't seem likely. Gabriel wouldn't be so slack.

'But you said you had,' she said.

'I said so, but it wasn't firm.'

The questions I was burning to ask were where Jo was, what had happened to her; but it wouldn't be any good asking them. There wouldn't be a sound answer.

She pushed her black hair into place and I saw a big ring on her finger, big enough for a poison ring. It looked old and worth quite a few roubles.

'The weather's becoming quiet,' she said, watching the sky. 'We could go by morning.'

'By morning by what?'

'The plane. It would still fly, wouldn't it?' She smiled. 'It's only thirty miles.'

'Thirty miles can be a long way in certain circumstances.'

'But surely it's worth a risk?'

She put a hand on my shoulder. I could see the blazing great ring catching the starlight in its stone.

It was then I had a weird instinct for the unusual.

I had the idea there was a radio in the ring, and that what we were saying was going out to the monitoring room. This was radio island, practically, and such small devices would be as nothing to Gabriel's engineers.

After all, this was a professional spy organisation we had dropped on. They lived by such electronic bugs.

'If it got off, it might get to Flamingo Bay. Or it might fall in the ocean. Surely he has boats here?'

'There are two fast boats in the harbour round the headland there. There's a lift goes down in the cliff.'

'Well, if we fell in the sea, then a fast boat would be picking us up. I wouldn't like to try and escape, and then fail. Gabriel would be nasty, perhaps.'

I imagined him chuckling as he listened to that bit.

'Why do you think the plane is so badly wrecked?'

'It had a rough time. It should be looked at.'

'But there might be nothing wrong apart from bullet holes?'

It kept surprising me how she spoke exactly as if she had been Jo, knowing the same details, remembering the same conversations we hadn't had.

'I think we hit a wing tip.'

'But it still would fly?'

'Perhaps. I don't know.'

'But you'll have to know in the end. There isn't any other way off the island for us, is there?'

Us! I laughed as she said it, but my amusement with her impudence didn't last.

'There must be other ways,' I said.

'But it is always best to find a way and then concentrate on that way. Not go around fuzzheaded with hope that something else might come along. The plane is there. You must make it your way of escape, as if there wasn't any other.'

'Suppose that was what Gabriel wanted me to do,' I said.

'How should I know what he wants you to do? My advice is to cut with him and go.'

'My idea is that if I cut with him I wouldn't have the chance to go.'

'That is why you must make your chance now. Go and see what the damage is. Then it will be ready when you need it.'

'There's probably a guard on it.'

She shrugged.

'There are probably lots of difficulties. What you have to do is deal with them one by one.'

When I first suspected that poison ring, I had the idea we were being monitored. At first I also had the idea she was trying to sound like Jo.

But now the form of the sentences she used was nothing like Jo's idea of speech. Nor, indeed, was the quiet philosophical reasoning behind it.

Jo was quick, hot, lost her temper if something stood in the way.

This woman would save her temper and use her combined emotions to get rid of whatever was in the way.

She seemed to be as powerful in determination as she was statuesque in form. She was like Brünhilde, which was a good enough name for her before I drove myself further up the wall, trying to keep in my mind the differences I had to remember between Jo and the Jo-type woman.

It was going to be necessary to remember what I had said to Brünhilde as distinct from what I had said to Jo. To get myself confused over this might well be to get myself hanged on the beach to encourage the others.

We walked slowly back towards the house veranda, and then she took her arm from mine.

'Come to my room later,' she said.

Then she turned and walked away across the terrace out of my sight round the jutting corner of the house.

When she'd gone I went back and searched around the bushes and the flower beds, anywhere that Jo might have hidden, or have been hidden.

There was no sign of her. Probably the idea of a substitution had been thought out so that it would have been essential for Jo not to have been able to appear.

The search left me empty and tense. They were playing some game with Jo, and I would have felt better if I could have worked out what it was.

If I could have worked that out, I might have guessed where she was and why.

As I went back into the house, Jim was tidying in the hall. I suspected he had been idling round, pretending to be busy just to be there when I came in.

He smiled at me.

'Where's Mrs. Mancini?' I asked.

'She went to bed.' He spread his hands out. 'Tired, she said.' He bent and polished a table top with a big duster. 'The storm has gone. It should be fine tomorrow.'

Then he straightened, shook out the cloth and jerked his head at the study door.

'Boss says to go in,' he said.

So I went in. Gabriel was almost lying

in a deep armchair, his legs outstretched in a great victory sign. His position gave him four chins instead of his usual two. He grinned round a big cigar.

'You have been thinking,' he said.

'Ruminating.'

'And looking round?'

'Of course.'

'But the quarters and the station are all — ' he pushed a hand backwards over his head, ' — up that way. You went the other.'

It was unpleasant to think I had been watched, but I must have known it before then.

'There was a Chinaman walking in the trees and I followed him.'

'Ah!' he sighed. 'Lee. He wanders. Never still. I am near sure it is him, but you must make certain.'

He watched me with slit eyes. He couldn't have had me watched too closely or he wouldn't have thought Lee the only Chinese on the island.

'I'm not satisfied with my hold on the cast,' I said. 'Just go over the personnel again, will you?'

So he went over them again, and they added up to the same as the first time.

'So there are only coloured girls and women?'

He nodded.

'No white women?'

'No. I have such visitors, of course, but there are none here now, save your companion.' He chuckled. 'You will drive Mancini mad. He loves nobody, but he is very jealous of what belongs to him, even when he does not want it. He probably will kill you. I have been thinking about that. When you go, I shouldn't go back to the Island. I should go home to England where they have a lot of police and terrifying laws.'

He chuckled again, but for a long time now, and a tear squeezed out of the corner of one fatty eye.

'And how does one get back to England from here without going to the Island?'

He made little circles in the air with his cigar.

'You fly to Carbago. That is a hundred and forty miles south-west of us. From there Cunard flies to London. West Africa and up from there, I believe.'

'Where does one get an aeroplane to Carbago?'

He closed one eye and watched me.

'What is the matter with Mel's?'

'It got shot, and I hit a wing tip coming in. Further I had a motor surge and suspect sand in the carburettor. It wasn't inspected before I left the Island. Otherwise all is well.'

He nodded and I suspected that he was pleased with this information, though he was too good an actor to show it.

'It can be put right.' He waved his cigar. 'Jim puts everything right.'

'You don't just want me to feel at home?' I said, taking a cigarette from his desk.

'My dear man, I don't care if you are at home or away once you have done what I ask you.'

'I don't understand how you have no small organisation to guard against spies. After all, your merchandise is worth big money.'

'Are you offering yourself to head such an organisation?'

He cocked his head and seemed interested, though I was inclined to laugh.

'No. I think it should already exist. For instance, how can you be sure who comes and goes from Shark Island?'

'We watch,' he said. 'There is closed circuit television and radar.'

'You mean the television watches the beaches, the radar the air and sea, way off?'

'Roughly that,' he said.

He sat up and stretched his arms.

'I am tired,' he said, yawning. 'You will excuse me. The hurricane, keep coming back, has stolen a lot of my sleep.'

He grabbed the arms of the chair and jacked himself out of the seat. He nodded, left the cigar to burn out in a tray then went out.

That left me nothing to do but go to the room of my unexpected mistress. Only I digressed.

★　★　★

I went to my own room first to get my gun which I had hidden in the bed, on the underside of the top mattress indeed.

150

Of a nervous disposition in places like this, I walked in to the room as far as it enabled me to look behind the door. No one was there, and I closed it. Then the man walked out of the bathroom.

He had a Mauser in his yellow hand, and he held it very steadily, high, so that he could aim accurately right at my head.

He didn't bother about any melodramatic preliminaries like telling me to stand still or keep my hands in view.

He just said: 'My name is Lee. This gun is loaded.'

All the necessary information being given in the shortest cleanest way. Then he stood there and his dark, narrow eyes were very steadily measuring me up, physically and mentally.

'I'm glad to meet you, Mr. Lee. Take a seat. Let me have your coat and gun.'

'You sit down Mr. Blake. We have some talking to do.'

'What could we have in common?'

'You have been hired to kill me.'

'Then what we have in common is the wish that you remain alive,' I said. 'I'm not here to kill anybody. It isn't my line.

Do I look like a hired gun?'

'You are big enough not to need a gun.'
His eyes were very narrow, very steady.

'My life is a constant struggle with
arthritis. I can hardly move a joint
without acute pain. I can assure you — '

'Please stop talking and keep away
from the bed.'

I shrugged and sat on it, my back half
turned to him. I saw his finger tighten on
the trigger and for a moment I thought I
would get his first bullet, but he changed
his mind.

I eased off, a new lease of life making
my feelings shoot up with new hope.

'State your business, Mr. Lee. I can
assure you I shall be most interested.'

He ran his left hand along the top of
the gun softly, as if petting it.

'You come from Mel Barney,' he said.

'Yes.'

'He gave you a message.'

'No, he didn't.'

'There was a message!' He batted that
one out with a kind of controlled
violence.

'He told me to be careful of his aircraft.

What else should he say to me?'

'He gave you a message to pass, at Flamingo Bay.'

I shook my head and looked as helpless as I could.

'I don't know anybody at Flamingo Bay.'

I was worried then, because he didn't go on arguing or accusing. He just stood there looking at me as if his eyes were shut, only I knew they weren't.

'Are you mistaking me for somebody else?' I said. It was a gambit, but suddenly it struck me that it might have some substance in it. I had tended to forget the story of my double. 'I've been on the Island a fortnight. A tourist only. A surveyor from London. These dramatics are new to me. My life is a long way from ever seeing a gun pointed in anger.'

Whether he was swayed by this innocence I don't know, and his face never showed any alteration. Perhaps another Oriental might have detected a change, but to me, as Confucius said, they all look alike.

'I see we are not going to agree easily,'

he said. 'Did Gabriel tell you I am spying on him?'

'Judging from your performance he would seem to be right.'

'He is wrong. He is driving me into a position where I shall not be able to get out. Then he will say, 'Ah, he is a spy and we must get rid of him'.'

'But he says that now. You just said you knew that.'

'Then he *has* said it to you already. So far we get. He doublecrosses me. You realise he does the same to you?'

'I'm not expecting anything else. After all, he is in a unique position of power, and that will twist a man's mind.'

I slid off the bed. He fired and the bullet ploughed into the rich-deep mattress. I got my gun and when he appeared at the corner of the bed I shot at him and missed.

But although he wasn't hit he went back, so unused to the advantage his gun could give him, he didn't use it but went to protect himself.

I didn't want him dead or badly hurt. I wanted to preserve him.

The best way to do it was to abandon the gun play. I threw myself at full length and got his legs with one arm round his ankles. He went down face to the floor. In the effort to save himself he dropped the gun altogether. He just wasn't used to having one.

But he wasn't slow, either. As I got up on all fours and went to fix him down, he twisted over and wormed away across the floor so fast I couldn't get a real grip on him.

Then he kicked me in the face, but thankfully he wore soft shoes, perhaps for quietness.

The fight was on then, but he was so quick and slippery in his escape twists that it was like trying to get hold of a lizard.

In the end I just drew back and hit him as he made another attempt to dodge my grip. It was a good stroke and got him just at the right instant. He went backwards on to the bed and swung his feet up to turn the fall into a somersault to the far side of the bed.

But his act was rather like a chicken

running about with its head cut off. He was out cold, and he must have lost his automatic reactions just as he was half-way up his loop.

He got over, but collapsed and crashed to the floor in a heap on the far side of the bed. I got both the guns from the carpet and went round to him.

He was sitting with his back against the bed, his head twisted and I thought for a moment that the worst had happened. But it hadn't.

He opened his eyes after I got a cold wet sponge from the bathroom and smacked his face with it.

'Can you hear me?'

He didn't answer for some time, as if he was only half with me.

While he was bringing his senses into line, I kept looking at him and thinking he was like Simpson. Even the fact that they all looked alike didn't dissuade me.

The idea struck me that Lee could have been innocent, but that Gabriel had somehow seen Simpson and got the two images mixed.

Then it occurred this idea came only

after I had already been thinking of my own double, and you can get persuasive trains of thought that mislead.

'Have you got a brother anywhere, Mr. Lee?'

'Five and three sisters,' Lee said, feeling his face gingerly. He had very small delicate hands.

'Back in Hong Kong?'

'They move around,' he said, as if the matter was of no interest. 'Mr. Blake, you are very impulsive. This time it will do no good. You cannot win against me, I think.'

'Tell me why.'

He watched me steadily.

'I know where the woman is.'

It connected like an electric shock.

'Mrs. Mancini? Where is she?' I got hold of him and started shaking.

'You can do no good! Let go!'

His shrill voice stopped me, and brought some common sense to bear. I let him go.

'I am alone here,' Lee said. 'I must watch for myself, trade with what advantage I have.'

'What do you want in exchange for

telling me where she is?'

He stiffened as he sat against the bedside. A moment later someone knocked at the door.

I straightened up. Lee just sat there, watching me, but hidden by the bed from anyone who came in. He drew his legs up underneath him. It was lucky he was so small a man.

'Come in!'

The door opened and Brünhilde came in, smiling with regal self-assurance. I went round the bed to her.

'I thought you were lost,' she said.

'Only when I'm with you,' I answered. 'I had a lot to talk about with G.'

'What have you decided to do?'

'I'm not sure. He talked about how easy it will be for me to go.'

'Until the time comes to try. Don't listen to him, Johnny. I told you there is only one way off this island — the plane.'

I went by her to shut the door and looked up and down the wide corridor outside when I did it. I was worried about anyone listening out there, but I had already accepted the fact the place was bugged like a monkey.

'He said he would get it repaired for me.'

'Don't believe anything he says. Get out.'

'I can't believe anything anybody says,' I said, and looked straight at her.

'That is the best way to be for a man in your situation,' she said and smiled slightly. 'But just for the time being I have a confession to make.'

'That should be interesting,' I said. 'In fact, I don't doubt what you'll say will have an interested audience outside this room, so don't keep your voice down.'

Then she laughed shortly.

'You know the game, don't you?' she said.

'I know the bugging game,' I said.

Suddenly she held out her hand and showed the ring. Then with her other hand, she opened it.

'So right am I,' I said. 'A device.'

'A jamming device,' she said, clicking it shut again. 'No bug will work within fifty yards of this spot. Not only does it jam, but it spreads the mush so that it is impossible to get a direction fix on it. At the present, every microphone in this building is being jammed out, so that, as far as the monitors are concerned, the jamming could be happening in any one of forty rooms, or outside the house altogether.'

'What about in the radio room itself?'

'That is a large place, and shielded,' she said.

'You know your wireless, sweetie,' I said.

She held the ring up again.

'You'll trust me?' she asked.

'I might as well,' I said. 'After all, I don't know your game. It might help me.'

'That is, of course, the object,' she said. 'Let me tell you now — '

I caught her wrist.

'Why not in your room?' I said.

Her eyes hardened, as if it was she now who was not doing the trusting. But all this time Lee had been sitting silent and hidden by the bed, listening to everything we had said. He formed a large bug, and despite the fact Gabriel was at the moment against him, you never could tell how these spy elements could switch when it paid.

So far little of importance had been said. Bug-jamming devices are getting common now, though not all as good as Brünhilde's. Lee must know already that I knew the woman, and that I was not quite the poor surveyor from London I had said.

Thinking back I couldn't think of anything said which could help Lee in the slightest.

That was one worry out of the way. Two more remained.

It was essential to hear what Brünhilde had to say; more essential still to find out from Lee where Jo was.

The situation then was that if I went with Brünhilde — and I didn't see how I couldn't — Lee would be free to go with his information intact, our bargain unstruck.

If I didn't go with her it was likely I would be sunk within the hour, because that was the kind of girl she was. At that time, all I was able to think was that she was of the Shark Island establishment playing, for the nonce, some game of her own.

But she could switch.

There was, of course, a third way. I could introduce my visitors to each other. That would be fun, but the sort of fun like a bonfire when it suddenly gets out of control.

Looking at her I realised it was getting out of control anyway. Something about my suggestion had put her in a blazing temper.

'You *are* Jonathan Blake, aren't you?' she said between beautiful teeth. 'Don't say there has been a mistake with that piece of waste material from Montego Bay.'

'I have never been to Montego Bay. And do you know what? I don't believe that there is a double. I think it is something that has been made up to confuse.'

I seemed to hear Lee's muscles straining as he tried to get a good earful.

'Do you know what I think?' I went on. 'I think that this double from Montego Bay has been invented. I think a tale has been invented that he is in with some gang. I think that the reason is that it has been planned that I, being mistaken for a non-existent double, will be handed something of great importance.'

She stared at me.

'Johnny, you're mad. How could that benefit anyone?'

'I hope to find out. But, you see, my arrival in the Caribbean has aroused considerable underground interest. I don't know why. But there could be a reason. I was known about, and it was decided that I could be suitably split into two, for a reason yet to appear.'

'Why on earth should you think this?'

'Gabriel knows all about me. I've been investigated, you might say. My arrival was expected and the story of a double put about — obviously after I'd got to this part of the world. There couldn't be any point in it before.'

'If there is any point in it at all!' She tried to mock, but she was tense and watchful.

I knew that Lee, behind the bed, was as tense and watchful. I began to feel that I had hit upon the solution to my dilemma. The introduction was being effected by a common fear, which could affect each in a different way.

'Let's get on, perhaps the point will appear, sweetie,' I said. 'There was one flaw in all this idea, which is that there happened to be one man — and an important man to Gabriel — who knew me.'

'Mel Barney?'

'He was drunk when I got there. Between seeing him days before, he'd been fed this story of the double. A double with a bad tale of violence attached. So he held me up. Then he knew it was me, and then he said there couldn't be any other.

'I don't think Mel believed the story from the start, but he had to try because somebody was putting the pressure on him.

'That was why he was drunk. Because he couldn't make up his mind. And because he thought I was running into a murder trap, which, in fact, I was.'

'If you're such friends that he would drink himself to death for your safety, would he do that to you?'

'You have a man's sense of malice, sweetie,' I said.

'The point about Mel is that he might have had no choice.'

'He gave you the wallet, didn't he?' she said.

Now we stayed still in silence. The woman knew everything. The only way I could see that she did was from Jo, and to tell everything Jo must have been forced.

I didn't care to think of Gabriel's methods. I felt they might be old-fashioned.

Then impulsively, like the fool I am, I defended Mel where it seemed the thing I wanted most to do.

'There was nothing in the wallet,' I said.

'Let me see.'

The smooth words came from the doorway. Gabriel stood there his hand out.

'Sorry, G.,' I said. 'I threw it away.'

7

'You threw it away?' Gabriel said. 'Where?'

'I chucked it out of the aircraft window.'
'When?'

'When we were over the sea. We were driven away from the strip at Flamingo Bay, so I decided to look in it and see how important it was. There wasn't anything there.'

He put his head on one side like a fat, evil parrot and looked at me.

'Someone's doing a lot of lying around these parts,' he said quietly.

'Lying?' I said. 'Why in hell should I lie about an empty wallet?'

He shrugged and came further into the room. I wondered how he had got the door open so silently when we had been there talking; but perhaps we had been louder than we had realised.

The situation, for me, was unmanageable now.

Lee was crouching on the far side of the bed, suspected as a traitor by Gabriel. If Gabriel found him, he would surely connect up Lee the traitor with me, and I would become also an enemy.

So for the moment I had to weigh Lee as being technically on my side, for he was staying hidden in the hope of not being seen by Gabriel.

But what of Brünhilde, standing in magnificent and watchful silence? Of which side was she?

She had posed as Jo, and somehow got to know everything that I had done in the past few hours. She could have been briefed by Gabriel's constant listening service.

Or she could have been briefed by Jo!

That was a shattering, but hopeful possibility. Unfortunately this was no time to ask and find out.

So I had one certain, one very uncertain and dead uncertain in the room around me. I decided to play a little time and see if my position could be improved.

There was no one in the open doorway

behind Gabriel, and I was sure Brünhilde's ring was jamming all outgoing signals in the way of loose talk. Possibly, because of the success of that instrument, Gabriel had been reduced to listening at the door.

'It would help if you told me what was supposed to be in that wallet,' I said.

Gabriel snapped his fingers impatiently.

'Valuable information,' he said.

'Was it meant to get here?'

'Eventually. Not directly. It would have been too obvious if Mel Barney had come direct. He was meant to drop it at Flamingo Bay, from there it would have been brought by supply boat later.'

'Why didn't Mel fly it there himself?'

'He obviously wriggled when he found the chance that you would do it.'

'That's not like Mel.'

'It shows he is being watched,' Gabriel said. 'So he, in your parlance, made a rapid pass across the goalmouth, leaving the backs concentrating on the wrong man.'

'There was no one at the airfield.'

Gabriel sat on the edge of the bed and looked at me with his eyes almost shut.

'Are you sure you remember that?'

'No,' I said. 'Now I come to remember, there was an Anglia kept going by on the road outside. It belonged to a millionaire called Harz.'

'Ah!' Again Gabriel snapped his fingers, but this time as one hitting on something. 'Harz! yes that could be. There are four of them in a syndicate.'

'I know them all,' I said. 'I played poker with them.'

'Why did they pick you?'

'Because Mancini wanted to get me away from his wife.'

Gabriel shook his head slowly.

'No,' he said. 'Something more than that.'

He was not contradicting, just thinking.

'What was in the wallet that they would want?' I asked.

'They play the markets,' he said, and sighed. 'If they get wind of a new small war or a revolution, they buy up steel, aircraft, arms shares, sell when the news breaks and clean up whether there is a war or not.

'The trouble with such men,' he said,

sighing again, 'is that they are sometimes not satisfied with the number of wars and risings in the melting pot, so they take a hand in the business themselves. Professional stirrer-uppers, I think you call them.'

'And this wallet had news of some new outbreak?'

He shrugged.

'There was a report which showed a trend that could be exploited, as far as they are concerned. As far as I am concerned I could use it to influence the greater nations to create a balance of power more to my wish. I make nothing when the wars begin. I make it when they can be kept on the edge for a few weeks.'

'And these brink ventures involve the lives of thousands — could be millions.'

'Don't let's have any English sentimentality. It's as false as their stiff upper lips.'

He was thinking again. So was I. I had a gun in each trouser pocket and felt weighed down at the hips like a Western baddie.

The feeling that this was the moment to act, if there was to be a moment at all, got me right in the spine. I looked at him, pondering on the bed.

'Gabriel, I'm sorry. You've been nice so far, but I can't risk it any longer.'

I clunked him with my right as he sat. It was no question of missing, for he was a sitting target, and I get a fair amount of practice in at the club.

He just grunted and went flat back on the bed. I got my left hand in my pocket and turned on Brünhilde, ready in case she was fast on his side.

But she was looking at me, with amusement, or excitement, shining in her eyes. Then she went and shut the door.

'Get some towels out of the bath, Lee,' I said.

The little Chinese got up, glanced briefly at the inert lump on the bed, then went into the bathroom. He came out again and I made a sound job of Gabriel. Brünhilde gave a hand.

When Gabriel was fast and muffled, I humped him into the built-in wardrobe and slid the doors across. Lee watched in silence. Brünhilde just smiled.

'It should be interesting now,' she said.

'Even if Jim assumes G.'s gone to bed, he will go to wake him at 6 a.m. So that you have, with luck, five and a half hours to get off the island in the face of a constant television watch and a Land-Rover patrol which has the magic box right on its dashboard.'

'I didn't know about the Land-Rover. The TV can be fixed.'

'If a screen goes blank they send to find out why.'

'One's not going blank. I said fix it not wreck it.' Then I turned to Lee. 'Where's Mrs. Mancini?'

He smiled, very slowly.

'First there is a bargain.'

'Well, what is it?'

'You get me off the island. I'm not safe here any more.'

'It's but little you ask,' I said sarcastically. 'I don't know that I can get myself off.'

'There is a plane?' Lee said, still grinning.

'Will it carry four?' Brünhilde asked.

'Four?' I said, swinging round on her.

'Four,' she answered firmly.

'I doubt it'll get off the ground. It's sick.'

'We try, then,' said Lee. 'It can only fail.'

'It can fall down and drown us all.'

'If we stay,' he said, shrugging, 'worse. Much better to drown.'

This cheering item was a piece of philosophy based upon known facts. Brünhilde was amused by it, or seemed to be. Once again I began to doubt what side she really held.

'The aeroplane is the best,' Lee said. 'For it happens there is not one on Shark Island but yours. Gabriel does not fly.'

The matter was of no importance. I was not concerned much with pursuit in the air. I was primarily concerned with getting into the air.

In my vivid imagination I could see myself holding the throttle bang open and tearing across the rather limited sand waiting hopelessly for the lift to begin, with the rocks coming nearer and nearer ahead of me.

I am coward enough to think there must be an easier way than just killing yourself.

'Where is Mrs. Mancini?' I said, squeezing the vision of the pile-up out of my head.

'You bargain?' Lee persisted.

'All right. If we can get off, you'll be in it. Promise.'

'She is in the room by the watch room,' he said. 'Staff on all night. Difficult to get at her.' He shook his head. 'Shouldn't think you would get her away.'

'Gabriel wants to see her,' I proposed.

'You have not a written note,' Lee said. 'There is always a written note from Gabriel.

'Gaby is a born torturer,' I said. 'Give me the layout of the radio wing.'

It seemed there was a door at the end of the corridor outside the bedroom which led into the work wing. In the work wing there was a machine room at the far end, the monitoring room in the middle, and a rest room nearest us. On the other side of the passage there were two filing rooms and a roomful of tapes and teletypes, where a duty typist was always on, putting black and white tabs on everything that came in.

Jo was held in the typist's room.

The door from the house to the work wing had an alarm which went off if the wrong combination was used on the door lock, and which locked every other door in the wing until an all clear was received.

'The door is steel,' Lee said. 'Only Jim and Gabriel have the combination, and the two keys which are also wanted to open the door.'

There was a silence.

'Has anybody tried this door before?' I asked him.

'Oh, yes. It has been tried,' Lee said, nodding. 'With most unfortunate results.'

'Is it the only way in?'

'Yes. The only way.'

'Then it must be opened at change of shift?'

'Indeed. At 2 a.m., 10 a.m., 6 p.m. Jim usually opens the door then.'

'By himself?'

'With the three for next shift, and four guards. They are a lazy lot, the guards, but they have automatic rifles which are issued just before and taken back to the gun room just after.'

'That girl's been nothing but trouble for you,' Brünhilde said, charmingly.

'Can the door be opened from the inside?' I asked Lee, ignoring the big woman.

'No. But there is a vent shaft. It is a weakness. Nobody speaks of it to Gabriel in case it might be useful one day. It is an oversight. All prisons have some detail men forgot, but others have time to find.'

'The vent can be opened from the inside?'

'Yes. Only from the inside. It is at the end of the passage and comes out above the roof of the garages.'

'I'll get you off the island, Lee,' I said, 'but only if you open that vent for me.'

He stiffened.

'It would be death for me to go back there!'

'It'll be death if you don't.' I showed him my gun. 'Surely it won't be that difficult? Put yourself on the next shift and you're in.'

'I am not on shift.'

'Put yourself on.'

'But there is a man detailed — they would notice — No.' His rigidity went and left him passive. 'No. It is easier to die now.'

Damn the Oriental psychology. But the more I thought of it, the more logical Lee's view became. Why should he go to extra effort to obtain the same end product — his death?

★ ★ ★

Brünhilde broke the silence with some of that easy assurance of which she was mistress.

'Mrs. Mancini wouldn't be in danger if she stayed,' she said. 'Now that the wallet is lost, Mrs. Mancini is the next best thing for Gabriel.'

'Why?'

'Because once Gabriel publishes the fact she is here, the Syndicate will have to try and get her back. I should think by paying.'

'No. I think my idea the best,' I said turning to Lee.

'But Jim will see me, and he will know so — ponk!' He made the gesture of pulling a trigger at his head.

When a lot of objections are slammed at you, at first the mind just stares at them and accepts a kind of defeat.

Then the mind gets a little angry at being frustrated, and after a while begins to see.

If the alarm went out of shift change hours, the guards would have no guns.

This measure was probably for Gabriel's self-protection, as he wouldn't trust the natives with his armoury except under supervision.

'All right, Lee,' I said. 'We'll do it this way. You try the door, sound the alarm and then run back here.'

'Are you crazy?'

'No.'

'The whole house will be alive with people!'

'How many guards sleep in the house?'

'Four. Always four.'

'They have no guns?'

'They have knives.'

I remembered the wide-bladed billhook Simpson had tried to slice my head off with. Such knives were certainly an argument for good behaviour.

'You seem to suffer undulations of

supreme optimism and practical pessimism,' Brünhilde said. 'Gabriel has the key to the gun room.'

'It's the knives I worry about now.'

She took a cigarette from the box and lit up. She walked over to the cupboard wardrobe, then turned back, changing her mind.

'I could sound the alarm,' she said, sweetly. 'Then, when Jim and the guards come, I can shoot them some line that will hold them a little. You go into the arms room and wait for them to go back. They go in, you wait behind the door. They stack the rifles, then you hold them up from behind. Then you have the guard and Jim.'

'Jim does not go in with them,' Lee said. 'He stands back by the door where there is a gas switch. If he presses the button gas sprays in the arms room, and the men are knocked down as instantly as makes no difference.'

'Gabriel seems to trust machines rather than men,' I said.

'Very wise,' Brünhilde said.

'How would Jim know who you are?' I

said sharply. 'There's supposed to be only one white woman on the island. Yet Gabriel didn't look surprised to see you.'

'Gabriel never shows anything.' Her soft voice had a sharp edge, as if, perhaps, she didn't like Gabriel.

Lee touched my arm, and I reacted as if to knock him back where he had started from, but he whispered in time.

'Someone going by outside.'

His eyes flicked to the door. Brünhilde stood quite still, watching me. I went to the door and opened it even as quietly as Gabriel must have done.

The sound of soft footfalls was clear out there, though they beat on the carpet as deep as a lawn. I looked towards the left, in the direction of the work wing.

Three men were walking along towards the ordinary looking door at the end. The two nearest me were blacks, and their attitudes suggested they held automatic guns in front of them. Ahead of them was Jim. They walked fast.

Near the door, Jim made a signal without looking round. His guards stopped and he went on alone. He did something to the door that I could not see, and in a few seconds, it opened.

Jim went on through. The guards hitched up again and followed. The door stayed open behind them.

This open door was a surprise and a pointer to the fact that Jim would be instantly coming out again.

The pause was not long. In about forty seconds, he reappeared with the two men behind him.

In front of the men and behind Jim was Jo.

My heart quickened up. Something had made them change their minds about keeping her in the strong room wing, and whatever it had been, it hadn't been Gabriel.

This made it look as if Jim acted on his own initiative when he felt it to his advantage.

I kept the door to a mere slit as the little party went by. Opposite me they turned and went down the stairs.

At the bottom they turned left and went into Gabriel's study. I saw the door pushed to, but not shut fast.

'What was it?' Brünhilde said.

Something in her attitude made me wary.

'A guard patrol,' I said. 'Is that usual, Lee?'

I forget what he said. The answer didn't matter anyway.

'Hang on here,' I said.

Outside on the landing it was quiet, but I could hear air conditioning fans hushing somewhere. I closed the door behind and went down the stairs.

The hall was empty. From the study I heard some soft voices, but too faint to hear what they said. I pulled my revolver from my right pocket and crept on to the study door.

'You refuse to say, then?' Jim said.

'Yes.' Jo sounded calm.

'But, look, I'm doing you a favour. I'm not Gabriel.'

'I just don't trust you.'

'Who trusts anybody?' Jim said and laughed. 'I am making a business proposition. Ready cash. Now, you tell me where to find him and you get the bonus. Also you get away from here and do what you like. That is a good offer.'

'Right. Then I'll tell you. I don't know where he is. So far as I know I never saw him.'

'So you might have seen him and not known?'

'I think I would have known, however alike they were. Yes, I'm sure I would have known.'

'Let me tell you what I hear,' Jim said. 'I hear the man was in Flamingo Bay, and I hear he flew behind you and crashed on the beach and ran away into the forest with a rifle.'

There was a silence.

'The man who ran from the wreck?'

'The man who tried to shoot you down. That one.'

'You mean the two are on the island now? This island?'

'Of course this island. You see the game. If he shoots your plane down, Jonathan Blake is dead but Jonathan Blake goes home to England and scoops the pool.'

I listened with considerable interest to this dialogue. My own belief was still that there was no double, that it was an invention created for a purpose I couldn't fathom.

But if I was wrong, and my double was indeed armed and hiding from me still, then a different and interesting situation was developing.

'It would explain the curious idea of the air fight,' she said. 'But the Australian put us there, using an empty wallet for the purpose. Is he in against Blake?'

'Mel Barney is hard up and worried,' Jim said. 'When a man gets so, he can be got at.'

That made me angry, but there was nothing I could do about it, though for a moment, the crazy idea did enter my head to rush in and hold the lot up.

Common sense switched my mind to defending Mel, and there was only one way to do it.

There must be something in the wallet after all.

The damn thing was hidden in my room. I hadn't wished to be carrying it around in case of any tricks by Gabriel, but the mere fact that I had kept it seemed to justify my idea then.

Jo spoke again, but more quickly now.

'I still don't see what this has to do with my husband.'

'Your husband is broke, Mrs. Mancini. I have now had confirmation that the cash he made over to you can be taken from you by British law. He was badly advised. It was a waste of money, lawyers and paper.'

'He never said anything.' She sounded stunned. 'It was a gift. Why does the law want his money?'

'Wholesale tax evasion. There are other liabilities amounting to a million and a quarter sterling.'

She said nothing now.

Very gently, with the tips of my fingers I eased the door in a little until I could see the large gilt mirror on the wall facing Gabriel's desk.

I found myself looking at Jim's profile, and facing him, and behind him, the door, was Jo. They were both sitting. One of the armed men leant against the wall behind Jo, chewing slowly and looking half asleep. I couldn't see the other.

Most likely he was behind Jim's back.

That would be the traditional bodyguard position, which would put him just on the other side of the door from me.

But I couldn't bank on that. He could be dead to the right of the door, ready to fire the moment the door really started opening.

'Gabriel wants the wallet,' Jim said. 'Mr. Blake has it, yes?'

Jo hesitated.

'I don't know.'

I saw Jim smile.

'It is very important to remember that in this industry a great many things of value lie about, but not everybody understands why they are valuable. The wallet is one. The phony Mr. Blake is another. I think you must know where they both are. Isn't it so, sister?'

'I remember seeing the wallet, when it was given to Mr. Blake. I don't know what he did with it. There was nothing in it. He probably threw it away.'

'I don't think he did. He is not a stupid man.'

Jo sat there, took a cigarette and didn't say any more.

'You clam up?' Jim said, smiling. 'Well, that's all right. We can wait a long time. An hour, perhaps two. At the end of that time, you unclam. That is not a suggestion. It is a fact that you will.'

He showed his teeth, and not in a smile.

I knew her too well to know she was hardening against him. Once she objected she could be as obstinate as a brick wall, and she was objecting now.

She would hold out as long as she could, and I felt that Jim would wait.

The only sounds behind me were the hushing of the conditioner fans. I turned and went back up the stairs and into my bedroom. Only Lee was there.

'Where's the woman?' I said.

'She went to her room.'

I got hold of his arm and steered him to the door.

'Just keep an eye on that door down there. If anything happens — anything at all, give me the wire.'

He hesitated before he said, 'Okay,' and went out.

I closed the door on him, then went to where I had slipped the wallet in behind the grille of an air duct. I unscrewed the grille with a penknife and felt so tense my heart didn't want to go on.

But the wallet was still there.

It was, as before, empty. I put the grille aside and carried the leather case to a light. I looked in every compartment, felt the silk linings of the banknote slots, but there was no scrap of paper.

Then I found the one thing I had, in fact, seen before and not attached any meaning to.

The wallet had a pouch in it for parking money and spare car keys. The pouch lid was snapped with a round brown button, a button that was loose.

My penknife went under it easily and I snapped the head off the brass under-stud. As it came off what looked like a fine coil of very thin wire came, uncurling, out of it.

Microfilm.

I had no means of blowing it up to see what it was about, but I didn't need to be told this was what everybody was looking for.

The cap went back on the button

easily. I closed the wallet and threw it on the bed. Then I opened a blade of my knife, put the tiny coil of film in the slot near the base where the blade didn't meet the framework and shut the blade again.

Lee's gun was still in my left pocket. I went over and put it in the air duct, then fixed the grille again, turning the screws with my thumbnail.

Then, from superstition, I went and slid the wardrobe door a bit, then stopped and looked back at the door outside which Lee was waiting.

It was still shut. I pushed the wardrobe wide open. Gabriel was still waddled up in the bottom, and I felt a bit sick with relief.

I don't know why I should have feared somebody had got at him, maybe because him not being there would have removed the value from my plan.

The plan was simple now. I had the means to buy Jo and myself off the island. I knew that what he wanted most was in my hands.

I bent down to him and eased the towel from round his mouth. He didn't open his eyes. I tapped his face to wake him. He didn't flicker anywhere.

For an instant I thought he was dead. Then I saw the vein in the temple of his bald head throb very, very slowly.

He was out cold, but it couldn't have been my whack that had done it.

The operator had been clumsy, probably in a hurry. He had drawn a spot of blood at the back of the neck where he had put the needle in.

The doors rattled when I shut them. The bargaining power had been taken out of my hands by Gabriel's not being able to take part. For to deal with Jim would be to rouse all Gabriel's vengeance when he did come to.

More than that, Gabriel had fixed everything with a double lock. The work wing had alarms, double locks; the gun room had double locks and a gas spray inside.

Could there be any doubt then that there was a double lock on Jim, however insolent and independent he appeared?

The trouble with a spy is you need a

spy to spy on him, otherwise what you get in merchandise is likely to be worthless or sold already.

I went to the door and called Lee in.

'The woman went to the cupboard?' I said.

He hesitated and then nodded.

'Didn't you watch her?'

'I was at the door. Here. I listen for you. I do not want you to go without me. You understand? You promised.'

'Even though they brought the girl out themselves? All right. I'll stick to it if I can on one further condition. That is, you stick to my side and do what I tell you.'

'What do I do?'

'You obey whatever I say. Okay?'

'Yes. Okay. You promised. I'll take that.'

'Right. It seems the woman gave G. the needle to give us more time. He will be out for some while, I think.'

The decision I was trying to make may seem small but it was hard. To help me, I wanted Lee to have his gun back, but though he seemed to trust me, I'm damned if I trusted him.

So I didn't tell him about it being

behind the grating. Instead I told him to wait just inside the door and if anybody came by surprise to get in behind the bed again, quick. It was more important for him not to be found than to try and fight. I'd already seen he wasn't much good at that on his own.

I smelt something was wrong as soon as I opened the door.

Brünhilde was there at the top of the stairs, coming up. As she saw me, she stopped dead, her eyes big, excited and still amused.

I looked through the banisters down into the hall; I saw Jim looking up at me. Behind him was one of his men with an automatic rifle. The guard was just raising it to take a sight on me.

'Look out!' Brünhilde shouted, coming to life again, 'They mean business!'

She ran the last step, on to the landing as I jumped out on to it. In a moment the bullets would begin to tear up the scenery round me and probably me with it.

I got Brünhilde right in front of me, breathless and beautifully ugly.

Then I bunched the hardest fist I ever made and I smashed it into her jaw. Her head jerked right back, something fell, she half twisted and then reeled backwards down the stairs.

8

The main thing I noticed about Brünhilde when I smacked her in the jaw was that she didn't look surprised. I had a split second to be grateful my hunch had been right.

She went back on to the next stair and swung against the wall. Below I saw Jim standing looking up at me. One of his guards, just out of the study door behind Jim, had his gun ready. He seemed hesitant to aim any shots while Brünhilde and I were still entangled.

She ducked at me and tried to tackle my legs, but the hit on the jaw had slowed down her reactions and I stepped aside easily.

She straightened again, trying to keep her back against the staircase wall, and then I grabbed and pulled her over in front of me. I got in two short jabs, one to the belly and one to the head and she sagged.

She made a guard between me and the two men downstairs.

Jim shouted something tersely. Jo came out of the study doorway and the second guard was behind her. Brünhilde was leaning heavily on me then.

I got my gun from my pocket and, swaying together as we were, I took a pot at the leading guard's gun. I missed it but hit his arm and he dropped the weapon and yelled like blazes.

The second guard, instead of tightening up at this sign of attack, let his gun and his jaw fall together. The rifle hung in his hands as if he had lost all use for it.

'Scrum!' I shouted.

I slicked Brünhilde's wig off with the gun muzzle and swung it out over the stunned group below. Startled already by the firing, the eyes of Jim and the guard fixed on the flying wig.

Both ducked as it went sailing down.

Jo responded to my shout. She turned and saw her frightened guard staring upwards. She lifted her leg right up and drove it into his middle. He just collapsed about his navel, clasped it and the gun dangled heavily from his shoulders on its leather straps.

Jim twisted round to get the gun from the wounded man. He must have realised then the disadvantage of having these leather slings as part of the uniform. He wasted time in getting it over the groaning man's head.

By that time Jo was almost at the top of the stairs.

As she came up I pushed Brünhilde off me and gave a short left to the chest. Then I spun her and she went headlong down the stairs.

Jim started to shoot. Bursts of plaster flew out of the wall as the bullets spelt their way along to where we were. I got Jo's shoulder and helped her on her way over the top step. She went flat down and slid on the polished floor to the bedroom door. I dropped down on my knees.

We were both out of range of the guns below owing to the angle of the landing edge. The firing stopped.

'Why do you play this kind of game?' Jim called out from below. 'You stand no chance.'

'You haven't seen my cards,' I said. 'At the moment I have Gabriel and the wallet in hand.'

The only sound breaking the following silence was Brünhilde's gasping from the bottom of the stairs.

'You have G?' Jim said softly.

'I have G.'

'Safe?'

I thought of Gabriel bundled up in the wardrobe, but realised I didn't know if the needle prick had shot in dope or plain poison, except that he had been alive just now.

'Safe enough.'

Moving under cover of the newel post I could see down to where Jim stood, the gun in his hands but looking relaxed rather than threatening. One guard had sat himself in a chair to hug his arm. The other stood fumbling with his gun, unsure of what to do.

'We might do business,' Jim said.

His head turned slowly as he scanned the landing to try and catch a sight of us.

'We might at that,' I said.

Jim snapped out orders to one man to

go to the first-aid hut and to the other to go into the gun room and wait. It looked as if he was clearing the decks for personal action. Next I saw him go near Brünhilde as she hauled herself up.

Then, for the first time I thought I recognised 'her'. The hair was bright yellow and even under the heavy make-up it slotted in with what I remembered Muck had looked like.

It gave me a shock, because it meant that Muck was a damn sight cleverer in following me than I was in running away.

Jim looked at the fraud a moment, then hit him somewhere in the side of the face with the gun. Muck went down, this time to sleep soundly.

Jim turned and looked up the empty staircase.

'I wish to talk,' he said.

'Leave the gun down there and come on up,' I said.

He hesitated. Then I saw him smile. He rested the gun against the stair wall and then began to come slowly up the stairs. I stood up. Behind me, Jo, got to her feet. Jim hesitated half-way up the broad flight.

I went out and sat on the top step, looking down at him.

'Talk,' I said. 'I want to be going fairly soon.'

He grinned and took a cigarette packet from one pocket and a lighter from the other. He held them up to show they were not weapons. I didn't suppose they were. If he had had a weapon on him I reckoned he wouldn't have wasted those valuable seconds trying to get a gun off the wounded man.

That hesitation had lost him Jo.

He lit up, then smiled.

'The wallet,' he said. 'I would like to see it.'

'Jo,' I called over my shoulder, 'It's on my bed. Would you fetch it?'

I heard her go on the soft carpet and come back in a moment. I held my left hand up over my shoulder and she put the leather case into it. I held it for Jim to see.

He nodded, his black eyes very bright.

'And G?' he said. 'Can you show him, too?'

'No. He stays where he is.'

Jim shrugged.

'You say he is alive?'

'Yes.'

'If anything should happen to him it might not be pleasant for me.'

'You mean he has some kind of double lock on you?'

'He has that on everybody. He has it so that if he died you'd surely die, too. He is a man of great power and charm.'

'If you feel like that about it, how can we do business?'

'It is believed the wallet was thrown out of your plane.'

'I see. So it could be useful to you, even under pressure of your enforced loyalty.'

'Oh yes, like that. Then we can do business?'

'I'm not interested in money. I just want to get away. Free access to the plane round about dawn.'

He shrugged.

'I can't guarantee any such thing. I am boss here — in the house. There are different arrangements outside. They are the ones who will look for G. if they suspect anything is wrong.'

'That is the Land-Rover patrol?'

'That is it. It has TV that can see any part of the beach around the island. Cameras are in the trees.'

'I heard about that. Yet all the same, people do land here and get away again without being spotted.'

Again he shrugged.

'Life is filled with mysteries,' he said. 'It is a fact that they do get on Shark Island, but they don't get off again.'

'I don't really see how we can do business along these lines. You have nothing to sell.'

'I can exchange the details of the island watches for that wallet.'

'But do you know them *all*? You said it wasn't your sphere of influence.'

'That's true, but — '

'Who *is* in charge of the patrol?'

'I don't know. G. keeps his departments sealed off, one from the other. So that each chief knows he isn't a top dog, and that somebody else can always come down on the back of his neck.'

'If you know so little why should I trust what you say you do know?'

'There is no one else to trust, is there? I can at least tell you the methods the patrol use.'

'And the times they use them?'

'There are no times. G. says fixed times are a trap.'

I looked past him to the sprawled figure of the disguised Muck.

'Is that man the one who came in the Piper?'

He was startled and looked round sharply.

'Him? No! It was the man like you!'

'There is no man like me. It's a fake cooked up by the millionaire's syndicate, back on the Island.'

He hesitated, then looked round to Muck again.

'But it couldn't have been him!'

'Why not? Do you know this man?'

'He works for G. But as a woman. I did not know he was a man.'

He turned and went slowly down the stairs. When he got by Muck he crouched, looking at him.

'The hair is dyed yellow,' he said. 'There is a lot of make-up. Lipstick slapped on. The mouth is different underneath. And the eyelashes, fixed and the brows — all what ugly women wear, but the face shape, you see. The bones — ' He gestured with his hands and then looked up at me.

'What's the matter?'

'It could be like you,' he said. 'If you took this makeup off, made the hair your colour, the eyebrow turned here — it could be.'

'But I saw this man in the hotel bar. He didn't look like me then.'

'Muck was like an actor whose face becomes stained with too much make-up. He can wear more and nobody notices. He can put the small touch here and there and then he is a different man. It is the small things that alter faces and the mannerisms that people know you by.'

He straightened up.

'This could be the man,' he said, pointing down. Then he grinned. 'Size for size, shape for shape. Perhaps he is not quite as tall as you, but who remembers an inch or two?'

How true when one thinks that often

people will say to someone. 'You've lost weight' or 'You've put it on a bit, haven't you?'

The two different things can be said to you in the same room within minutes of each other. The fact is, people don't really remember you in detail.

If Muck went back to England looking like me the business people he would see would probably say, 'Hallo! your holiday's shrunk you' or, 'you ate too much, I can see.' All the man has to do is agree.

'He works for G?' I said.

'As a woman,' Jim repeated.

'Why?'

'Perhaps he wanted to keep his manship secret so he could be you without G. thinking it possible.'

'What did he do for G?'

Jim shrugged.

'I know so much. I try to know more, but trying to see past G. is nearly impossible. He is too fat. He blocks off the view.'

'But did Gabriel set him on to me as the *femme fatale*?'

'Funny,' Jim said, cocking his head.

'But I don't think he did. The trouble with the people you have to hire is you don't know if they've finished with you or not. It's a poor business for goodwill.'

'Somebody cleared the Piper off the beach,' I said. 'Did anyone look at my plane?'

'We patched the bullet holes,' Jim said. 'We didn't try the motor. But I don't think it worth while trying that way, Mr. Blake. You could never do it.'

'What exactly are you offering to sell, then?'

'As I say — the way the patrol works. But I keep on telling you, the plane's no good. They'll be watching that.'

'What other way is there? A boat?'

Jim didn't answer but pointed down to Muck sprawled on the carpet.

When I saw what he was getting at I also realised that Jim was not just playing along with me a solo purpose game. He was going to level up some old outstanding scores at the same time.

I glanced round to Jo. She gave a slight nod. But behind her and out of Jim's sight stood the slight Chinese, Lee. He watched me intently.

'But,' I said, turning back to Jim, 'if I go as Brünhilde whatever happens to Jonathan Blake?'

'Whatever do you think happens to Jonathan Blake once G. gets round,' he answered calmly.

★   ★   ★

Sitting on the stairs, in control of the indoor situation, it was ribbing to think that it was only the indoor situation. Once I stepped outside the house another set of difficulties took over. Like Sisyphus, who kept pushing the rock to the top of the hill only to find it roll down again, I was getting sore.

There were ways to cheat the patrol but it was impossible to think of them without knowing what normally happened to start with.

I didn't trust Jim. I couldn't see what he would get by helping me. I couldn't see him selling the microfilm — if he ever got it — without G.'s assistance. If he ever tried such a thing, I reckoned he'd be sunk for good in the spy business. G. would see to it.

That switched my mind to the immediate. Why was he making offers, stalling time?

As soon as I began to think, I got to my feet. At almost the same instant I saw the armed guard who had been sent to the gun room, creeping along the corridor towards me.

He was behind Lee. Jo was close to me. Although he was going to spray death pretty liberally, and probably kill the lot of us, yet he started as if it really didn't matter.

How he missed, Heaven knows. I think he started to spray bullets at me, but Lee, being nearer to him on his left, and then Jo being farther but also to the left just jigged his sight, and until he started firing he hadn't got the line at all.

I shot him dead. It was one of my best shots, right in the head. But even as I fired it I knew it had to be good, because if it failed there would not be time for a second pot.

He went down as if he didn't seem to

mind, just slowly walked backwards, his head rolling until he collapsed and went down like a sack.

At that moment Jim sprinted for an open door beyond Muck. I would have got him, too, but Jo grabbed my arm and the shot hit the chandelier.

What it hit I don't know, but there was a sudden blaze, a loud explosion, and every damn light went out.

I gripped Jo's arm in mine and shoved backwards to the corner of the stair wall. It was a good thing to do because not five seconds later the gun downstairs blazed off again.

Jim had not gone far.

The bullets were slapping into the wall somewhere near. He was certainly spraying. The only thing was he wasn't counting shots.

I changed my mind about making for the bedroom immediately and pressed Jo against the wall round the corner of the stair wall. The firing stopped.

My guess was he had run out of shots. I flicked on my small keyring light and found the bedroom door. I bundled Jo inside and I could feel Lee close behind almost breathing down my neck.

A light blazed up the stairway as I closed the door.

I let Jo go and crossed to the french windows. I opened them and threw back the shutters. It was still brisk out there, but fine and clear, the moon high.

As I stepped on to the veranda I heard a siren going. It wailed and rose and fell. It was on a moving vehicle, apparently coming towards us.

I could see nobody in the garden below, but in this place you couldn't go by what you could see.

'What are you going to do?' she said.

'Get away from the house. Can you climb down there? There's a trellis all the way.'

'Yes.'

She got hold of her skirt at the hem and ripped it. I didn't know she was so strong. Her legs freed, she swung over the balustrade and shinned down the trellis with the clumsy eagerness of a schoolboy.

Lee was waiting close by.

'You go,' I said, and went back into the room.

It seemed wise to get the spare gun from behind the vent grille even if pursuit was then at the door.

The screws were loosely put in with my thumbnail and came out easily. Outside, the howling of the siren droned down into a dying growl as the vehicle halted somewhere by the front of the house.

The grille came off. I snicked off the little light and pocketed it, then got the gun out.

As I got it I heard people running up the stairs, their feet making a soft drumming on the thick carpet. I ran back to the door and shot the bolt.

The door shook as somebody tried it from outside. I went back across the room. There was shouting down in the garden. I stopped at the windows and looked down. There were three or four men down there, searching the garden, but they hadn't got anybody yet.

There was a crash as somebody shot at the lock from outside. Again the door was tried.

'He's jammed the door!'

Some voice I didn't know, shouted.

'Bust it in.'

Somebody charged it and the room shook, but the door stayed firm. Gabriel had had this house built to withstand storms both natural and human.

The moon was bright in the room. I looked at the wardrobe, then went to it and slid the door open. Gabriel almost tumbled out. I looked closely at him, but he was still cold.

The door shook again, twice, but still held out. There was some shouting on the other side of it. There were odd cries and whistles from out in the grounds.

It looked like a with-one-bound-Jack-was-free situation, but I couldn't think of how to start the jump.

The crashing at the door had stopped. Perhaps they had sent for a battering ram. The sounds from the garden didn't indicate they had caught anything out there yet.

'All right, now,' I heard Jim say. 'Put it right in the bottom panel.'

And then despair brought an idea. I

have a small, crude ability to mimic people's voices in short doses and providing the listeners are not being critical.

I used Gabriel's bronchial tones then.

'What the devil are you doing, Jim?'

There was a startled silence. I undid the towels binding Gabriel. He was like a wet sack, lolling about.

'That you, G?' Jim called through the panels.

'Who in hell do you think?'

I got G. into a chair and shoved him across the carpet facing the door, his back to the moon from the windows.

'Are you all right? Are you okay, G?'

'I shan't be if you bust in. Get me?'

Again a pause.

'What do you want, G?' Jim said.

'Get off.'

'You sure, G?'

'This bastard's got a gun on me. Get off!'

Then I said in my own voice, 'Take a look through the keyhole, Jim. He's right here.'

We waited. I stood so he would see the

silhouette of me holding a pistol to Gabriel's head. It was a tense wait.

'Okay, G.' Jim said at last. 'Okay!'

I heard voices and men moving away from the door. There were some orders shouted outside in the garden. After that the sounds of activity out there died away.

Well, one bound had gained a breather, and it did seem that Jo and the Chinese had got away, at least for the time being.

It was sheer luck, anyhow, for my imitations are not very good. They are, like Jim's idea of imitation, based on mannerisms, but helped by the thickness of the door and the fact that Gabriel would have growled anyhow, I had for the moment got away with it.

Back at the window I watched the garden carefully, but saw no more of the armed searchers. They had been called off — ostensibly. I had no doubt they hadn't just gone.

I had already had experience of Jim's rapid turn and turnabout methods of loyalty, but through all that, I seemed to get the main vein of doing what was best for Gabriel in the long run.

But this breather would be moments of redeployment for the enemy, and that was the time to take full advantage.

If only I could think of how.

Watching the garden was rewarding, for after a few moments I made out men hiding around under the trees. They hadn't gone far. Equally, I felt they weren't very far from the door outside.

There was a way I didn't think they were — the roof. But there wouldn't be any way off the roof that didn't lead to the defenders sooner or later.

My breather didn't seem to be doing much good, but like most other things, to make good you must take risks. The garden was a foolish risk. The moonlight was too bright.

That being so I considered the only other way and unshot the mortice bolt on the door. I opened the door a little. It was dead quiet outside and for a moment I suspected it, for something was missing.

Then I realised the vent fans weren't running, but then they could have been on one of the circuits I had blown. It was pitch dark out there. The shuttering which had been closed against the storm was still in place.

I could move around in the darkness of the house, perhaps, and I could find a way out of it, but the house was still surrounded on the outside.

I felt a little depressed then, for the house was surrounded, the beach was surrounded, the island was surrounded, and I felt shut in. It was as Jim had said, there wasn't a way out of Shark Island.

The silence out there was remarkable. It was the silence of emptiness. If anyone is hiding in the quiet, you can hear, to an extent, his living. There wasn't anyone round that door or on the landing.

When I stepped out it was hot. The conditioning system made a lot of difference which was felt when it was off. As if the house was gathering latent heat and would soon come to the boil.

Then from below I heard voices. They were soft but urgent. One was Jim's, the other I didn't know. I went to the balustrade to hear what they said.

'The girl?' Jim said.

'She must have got away. We found nothing out there.'

That made me feel better. I had a wild guess that Lee knew of Simpson's hidey hole and that they had gone there. If that was right they would be safe for a while, anyhow.

'What's to do?' the second man said.

'Think of a way round,' Jim said. 'He's got G. up there and he shoots to kill. I've heard about that before. This time he can hardly miss.'

'Why did G. bring him in, then?'

'There's somebody leaking gen here. G. wanted Blake to find out who.'

The other man hesitated.

'How does G. know?'

'He gets to know.'

'If someone is doing it, how does he get the gen away?' The second man was impatient, almost alarmed.

'That's what we want to know. It can't be under *your* nose, can it? Your patrol is a hundred per cent.'

'Sure. Hundred per cent,' the second man agreed. 'It must be getting off by radio. What else?'

'There are too many checks on that. The operators can't get at the monitor tapes and doctor them. The tapes show what goes out and in all the time. G. would know in a minute when he heard the tapes. No. It's getting out solid if you get me.'

'There's nothing getting past my patrol!' the second man said angrily.

'Okay, okay. Nobody said,' Jim snapped. 'Maybe it's being bounced off the moon with a flashlight. Get back to square one. What do we do now?'

'Get G. out.'

'The only way he'll come out is lengthwise if you try that,' Jim said.

'Who do you reckon is the leak?'

'Lee.'

'Ah yeah! Could be. Could be. Never did trust those Hong Kongalese.'

'Much better have a Spanish-American-Swede,' said Jim.

'Look here, you bastard — '

'Shut up! Listen!'

I crept back into the bedroom. Gabriel lumped there, hardly breathing. Whatever he had been shot with had some powers of the soporific. He could have been dead almost.

That gave me an idea. I went back to the landing rail.

'Don't do anything sudden, gentlemen,' I said, quietly but firmly. 'But I have news for you.'

There was a hissing whisper, then Jim's voice came up.

'Blake?'

'Who else? Remember you said you would do business?'

'You did?' the second man snapped. 'Why you cheap — '

'Cut it!' Jim said. 'What do you mean, Blake?'

'Supposing I did kill Gabriel? Would that help?'

There was a scared silence.

'You must be crazy,' Jim snarled. 'What good would it do?'

'Who would succeed?'

Again there was a silence. I imagined the two bosses watching each other, neither daring to answer the question.

'It doesn't arise,' Jim said.

'Perhaps it does,' I said.

'Do you mean he's dead now, for God's sake?' the second man shouted.

I didn't answer. It was very effective. I heard one man take a long breath.

'Are you leading me on, Blake?' Jim said. 'I warn you — '

'Look, would I be here, talking to you, if G. was alive at my back?'

There were more hurried whispers.

'I don't see why you should kill your trump card!' Jim said. 'That's the crunch, Blake. That's it.'

'But I didn't kill him,' I said.

'He's not dead!' the second man said. 'It's some kind of trick. Don't — '

'You say he's dead?' Jim said again.

'I say he's dead. But I didn't kill him.'

'Then who the hell did? You had him — '

'You've got the man somewhere down there. Herr Muck.'

'It's baloney,' the second man said. 'That means G.'s been dead an hour. You spoke with G. not a few minutes back. What's the matter with you, Jim? Softening in the head?'

'What's the point in arguing?' I said.

'Come up and see. One at a time and no guns. I have all the guns necessary for this expedition.'

There was hard breathing, some whispering.

'Okay. We're coming,' Jim said.

'The bedroom door's open,' I said, shoving it open with my foot. 'It's moonlight. I shall see you. You won't see me. No guns.'

'Okay,' Jim said. 'We're coming up.'

I waited in the darkness to the right of the doorway. Into the blue moonglow they appeared slowly coming up the stairs. In that light they would certainly think Gabriel was dead. His whole attitude looked like it. So long as they did not see the faint signs of life in him, the trick would work.

They got to the top of the stairs, Jim in front. He hesitated then crossed the landing to the open door. A man in white uniform came behind him.

And then, as they reached the door and Jim stopped, watching the 'corpse' every damn light in the house came on again.

9

Jim was in the doorway. The other man pushed him forward, determined to see more closely. It was at that moment the lights came on.

All three of us were momentarily blinded, but it meant just an instant's hesitation, then the men's attention went back to Gabriel.

'He's sure dead!' the second man said.

Jim did not reply. I heard Gabriel's face being smacked, and then I called to my aid my three-evenings-a-week-fitness hobby.

I got the rail in my hands, somersaulted over so that I came down to the floor below feet first, and from long practice, nicely timed to meet the floor boards.

Jim shouted. I heard them run to the railing, then I ducked in at an open door and ran through a long room. The shouts increased as the men came running down the stairs.

There was a door at the end, then an unlighted passage, then a window, shuttered as most of the others still were.

I got the window open and one shutter and then I saw someone behind me. Some small sound must have caught my attention, for when I looked round, the someone was still a few paces behind me and coming up quickly.

My action was quick but it didn't have to be much. I just spun to one side of the window so I was in the shadow of the wall and invisible to the oncomer.

He stopped. It was Muck, still in his woman's rig, but with his wig in one hand and a pistol in the other.

'Give it in, Blake,' he said. 'I want to come flying with you. It's too hot here.'

'Our previous arrangement stands for naught,' I said. 'I thought you were a woman then.'

'I still weigh the same.'

He was peering, trying to see into the shadows where I was. The shouting still went on somewhere in the area of the hall. They had not yet rumbled my direction. There were so many doors leading out of the hall, most of them open.

Looking aside a moment I got a slant through the open shutter to the garden. I saw a man's shadow under a tree, which made sure the grounds were still guarded.

'You fixed Gabriel,' I said.

'Not for long,' he said, still peering, 'He's due to surface any minute now.'

'Once he gets back to normal we'll never get to the plane,' I said.

'I can,' he said. 'G. thinks I work for him. You must have seen.'

'He certainly accepted you,' I said, glancing through the window again.

It was a question of weighing up millstones. Either I could slug Muck again and leave him and go out and run the gauntlet of the men.

Or I could take Muck and use him to get to the plane.

'The garden is full of them,' I said. 'If they know you, perhaps we could come to an understanding.'

'Okay,' he said. 'What?'

'I'll escort you down to the cliff path. You'll have to act along.'

'I am an actor.'

'Let's try, then. Come along to the window and stow that gun. Remember I've got one also.'

'Okay,' he said, and came towards the window.

'Put your hair on,' I said.

He put the wig on and brushed it with his hand.

'Why did they leave you to come to on your own?' I asked.

'There must have been a lot going on. Also, they don't know for sure how to treat me.'

'Where did you get the gun?'

'It was lying around in the hall.'

'Then it's empty. Lie it around again. You can't stroll swinging a gun in one hand.'

He clicked out the magazine, looked, then put it and the gun on a table. He went out of the window and I went close behind him. We went slowly along the veranda, and put on a good flirtation act, talking and laughing.

We got to the end of the veranda and went down the steps on to the terrace.

There we hung about a little while and talked so no one could hear and laughed.

Whoever watched from the trees must have got a clear impression of the supposed setup. Muck played the woman well.

No one interfered or showed that we were being watched. The surrounding silence was queer, as if they and not us, were doing the playing.

We moved down the terrace steps and on to the path that twisted down between the heavy trees. Still no watcher betrayed his presence.

There was also a lack of movement back at the house. This stillness I disliked most of all. I felt it meant that Gabriel had returned to full power and had taken command of the situation.

The silence, the apparent lack of interest seemed to indicate that the situation for Gabriel was an easy one.

Yet we got on to the path without trouble. It was possible the act was good enough to confuse the watchers, but I'm not that kind of an optimist.

An interesting angle was that this

runaway was being carried out in company with a man whose main object was to murder me — or see it done — and then go back home and grab my unexpected legacy.

There was little time from the tension of that slow journey to wonder what Muck would do in the end. But as long as he kept with me, and we got to the plane and away, he couldn't do anything to me.

It would appear that he was dependent on my safety.

No one seemed to be following. Now and again we stopped to talk, which gave us a chance to look around without seeming to, yet still nothing happened.

'I don't get this,' I said. 'If G.'s come to, they must be looking for me and you, let alone Mrs. Mancini.'

'I don't know what the hell's happening,' Muck said. 'It don't fit.'

The fresh wind following the storm had died down into a moonlit calm that was hot.

We stopped again as we heard the Land-Rover start up somewhere back by the house. There was a shout, and then the truck moved off. By the sound of it, it went away from us, and soon it was no more than a hum in the distance.

'The patrol,' Muck said.

'But why go the wrong way?' I asked. 'They must know we took this path.'

We stood and listened. The truck must have gone right over to the other side of the island, it was so faint to our ears.

'This is crazy,' he said, staring at the moon. 'We run, but there is nothing to run from. They all run the other way. What does it signify?'

'Perhaps G. has come to and is playing a small cat-to-mouse game. He might think that funny.'

'He doesn't waste time like that,' Muck said impatiently. 'He wastes very little.'

'Why did he want you here?' I shot at him.

He looked at me sharply.

'It's hot in this wig,' he said.

'Keep it on. Somebody may be watching.'

'G. said nothing about why,' Muck said evasively. 'He was to tell me tomorrow. I think he'd got something on me and didn't want to let it go too soon.'

'It could be that why they don't follow now is they think you'll take care of me.'

'Could be. But that's if G. still thinks I'm in with him. Don't forget, Jim saw the wig come off.'

'Women wear wigs.'

'Men don't hit them in the jaw with fists. Not your kind of man anyway.'

We walked slowly past Simpson's hidey hole. Muck gave no sign he knew anything was there. Nor did I.

Nearby we stopped and looked down over the bay, where I had stood before. It was a wide, silver strand in the moonlight and looked big enough to get a big jet off.

Far off I could see our plane pinned down under the cliff. There was no sign of anyone about it. The Land-Rover wasn't down there. The emptiness of the beach was sinister but still inviting.

'What's going on?' I said. 'One minute the house is in siege then the culprits go and nobody does anything at all.'

'They will,' he said. 'Don't worry about that. They will. The thing is not to get tensions waiting. G. is fond of doing that.

He says people answer more readily when they have been stretched.'

'Not a new idea.'

'Are we going to get to the plane?' he said, suddenly urgent. 'There is no one down there.'

'Mrs. Mancini should be down there, but as you say, there's no one.'

The important point now was to find out from the hidey hole if Jo was there with Lee. If they hadn't made it there could be a reason for not bothering too much about me. They probably guessed I wouldn't go without her. I was a little tied by the fact I thought her husband would kill her, in spite of what Jim said.

The other fact was I didn't feel like leaving her in any case.

Then I decided to risk Muck. As the whole business on Shark Island was for us a matter of risks, one more shouldn't matter much.

'Wait and keep watching the beach,' I said. 'I've got an idea, but it might not work. Just watch. If there is anybody down there, they're bound to move enough to be seen.'

'Okay,' Muck said. 'But look, I've no gun.'

'They know you. They trust you.'

'The hell with that — '

'You want to fly off, don't you? Well, shut up and keep watching that damn plane.'

He unbent, but unwillingly. He didn't trust me whatever.

I went back up the path until he could see me no more, then I wormed around in amongst the ferns and came to the outjutting rock.

The stone wouldn't shift when I pushed it. I looked back to make sure Muck hadn't followed, then I pushed and shoved, but I couldn't move it as Simpson had done.

It was a difficult situation because I dared not shout nor hang around too long. Everything around me was still, yet I could hear nothing from inside the tomb.

Simpson hadn't shown me a catch, and I couldn't see where there could be one. I shoved again, and still the stone stayed solid and unmoving.

There could have been a catch on the inside.

Around me everything was still as before but I decided to take a risk of being heard and struck two taps with the butt of my gun.

No answer came.

Before I struck again I listened but the sound I heard came from outside, somewhere up the path. It was soft, heavy, regular. I peered round the rock edge.

Coming slowly down the path was Gabriel, his white jacket flickering in and out of the tree shadows. He was alone, smoking a cigar. He looked as if he had not suffered a bent hair from his ordeal, but the speed with which he puffed his cigar betrayed anger.

The sight of him froze me. This, at last, was the man who ruled the island by personal power and splendid ruthlessness. This was the figure that held all his men in control. This was the man determined not to lose.

I hadn't any doubt why he walked down that path.

He was coming for me.

As he came slowly down the slope I got back in amongst the ferns. It was still difficult to see why he should come alone, why the patrol wagon had been sent in the opposite direction.

He came alongside the rock and then stopped. He took the cigar from his teeth and stood there in silence. Then he turned and looked behind him, making sure no one had followed. From that point he turned slowly on his heel, looking into the shadows all round him until he came to face the rock. Then he stopped.

He waited there a few seconds, then came forward to the rock.

His performance was strange. It was the furtive carefulness of the guilty that he showed. I should have thought him too powerful to be afraid of anyone seeing him.

He came to the rock and put his flat hand against it. I saw him strain in silence, and then step backwards. Then again he looked slowly round.

'Blake,' he said, very quietly. 'Jonathan Blake!'

I didn't answer. I couldn't make head or tail of what he was doing, but I suspected he didn't *know* I was there. He just guessed.

But while he waited for an answer, I saw the stone swing slowly inwards.

Gabriel went on looking round, then suddenly saw the black opening in the rock. He took a step towards it, and then drew back sharply so that he could not be seen from the opening.

A man came out, but in what way he came I'm not sure. He went headfirst to the ground, as full of life as a sack, and then just flopped over.

I could see by his attitude that Lee was dead.

I saw the stone swing shut slowly, respectfully, like someone raising a thoughtful hat as a funeral goes by.

★   ★   ★

I stood up. Gabriel looked at me.

'You did it after all,' he said. 'I thought perhaps you had defected.' Then he smiled.

233

There was no point in answering. Looking down on the upturned face I couldn't be sure if it was Lee or Simpson. From that doubt I was sure it was both; that there had never been a Simpson, just Lee. They all look alike to me and my views of Simpson had been brief and of the moonlight-flicker variety.

My anxiety then was to know who else was in the rock, with which the sub-question was closely tied: Who killed Lee?

This was important because it vitally affected Jo.

Gabriel touched his fat face.

'It's good I have a lot of padding,' he said. 'You are exceptionally strong.'

'But not at guessing,' I said, and bent to peer into the hole. The moonlight showed enough for me to see it was empty. 'Somebody was holding the stone shut.'

'Sure,' Gabriel said. 'It goes a long way back, I guess.'

'Are you guessing?'

'In one way. In another, no. It must go back a long way. I have just found that this is a way on to the island which cannot be seen by the watch.'

I took a superficial interest in what he said in case he dropped something important. What I was worried about was Jo. If she had run down some bolt hole, I was sure it hadn't been alone.

Now I see one can be sure of things, sure as when the man thinks the trap won't drop at his hanging, because it said so in his stars that morning.

'I think you were wrong about Lee,' I said.

He shrugged.

'Does it matter now? All the same, I disagree. What I want is men and a defensive brain. You have the brain. You were a soldier, too.'

'That was a brief interlude.'

'However brief, still valuable,' Gabriel said. 'Come with me back to the house, please.'

'I'm worried about Mrs. Mancini.'

'She is safe enough,' he said. 'I believe she is well able to look after herself. To go down there — ' he pointed to the hole, ' — would be like the rabbit going in and finding the ferret at home. Leave it.' He was suddenly grim and sharp. 'You can't win down there. It is prepared. Come to the house. There isn't much time.'

He turned and began to walk up the path. The one sensible thing to do was follow, especially in view of his almost friendly attitude, something I hadn't expected after pushing him in the jaw.

Besides, I suspected he knew about Jo and where she was. I was damn right at that.

Following behind Gabriel I looked back, but saw nothing of Muck. I thought then that he must be the spy G. had been after, and yet still I couldn't see him staying unsuspected. He was such a self-seeker surely he just spun to the richer wind. G. could have bought him if he wanted.

But Muck had been after me. Of course he could have worked as employee and freelance both together, if the targets weren't mixed up together.

We passed up the terrace and went into the house. I saw no guards hiding under the trees. We came into the study once more. It was empty.

'Where are the forces?' I said.

'Back in quarters. But not the patrol, of course. Now, first, Jonathan, tell me how you would have got away from here knowing, as you did know, that every point is watched by television cameras.'

He took another cigar. His attitude was wholly warm now, but very grave.

'I need your help very badly,' he added. 'People have been getting on and off the island recently, and they have done it unseen. There must be a simple solution.'

'I know of a way,' I said.

'The one you were to use? Tell me. You can ask for anything in exchange.'

I felt he meant it. He was an odd man for putting out sudden waves of sincerity when he felt like it.

'Where the plane is,' I said, 'is the west end of a beach, created by two horns of rocks pushing into the sea.'

He nodded.

'To the east,' I said, 'is a similar but smaller beach. If you looked to sea from the middle of either you would get almost exactly the same scene.'

He took his cigar out and hissed a word, 'So?'

'I was going to switch the lines of the cameras, blinding the one on the west beach, and joining that empty line to the camera on the east beach. You'd get two screens watching the same thing, but the scenery anyhow is so simple and alike that the chances are against anyone noticing in the watch room.'

He showed his teeth.

'I'm glad you came, Jonathan,' he said, grinding the cigar out. 'Let's go and see.'

We went out and to the safety door of the work wing. He opened it. We went through and into a monitor room where four men were at radio desks, all wearing earphones.

At one man's side there was a bank of a dozen TV screens. Each tube showed a view of the Island's beaches. The one with the plane in it was not there. I looked for the beach I knew and found it because it was the same picture as the one next to it.

There wasn't any point in saying anything. I just pointed.

Gabriel nodded then spoke to one of

the listening men. The man looked up, then shrugged and shook his head. Gabriel led me out again.

This time we walked out and he did not close the guardian door. I hesitated.

'Those men in there I can rely on,' he said. 'I have given them guns. You may depend on any one of them.'

'What about Jim?'

'Jim's a fool,' he said briefly. 'A gambler, but he is as loyal as a gambler's stupidity permits him to be. He has the carrot dream of a million dollars ever dangling in front of his pineapple nose. A crock of gold, and he sees rainbows every day.'

We came into the hall, and he stopped.

'There is a microfilm,' he said. 'That I must have, somehow, before dawn. You will give it to me, because if you don't, you'll die, and so will I. This is not a threat, but a statement of fact. You have been through a confusing maze on this trip. I can explain much of it to you.'

He walked on to the door.

'We shall go down and watch that beach.' He tapped his pocket. 'I have radio. You have a gun, I believe. So have I. The patrol is armed. I can trust them, but the rest I've had locked in their quarters. They've been bought.'

'You say it all with the emotion of a guide pointing out Westminster Abbey.'

'It's bad to be excited before battle,' he said. 'You will recall the millionaire's syndicate. They invited you to poker so that you could be filmed and the result given to an actor to impersonate you.

'The idea there was that you would disappear and he would take your place. He would then come here as Jonathan Blakc, knowing beforehand, that Jonathan Blake had been strongly recommended to me by Mel Barney.

'You see, I knew there was something going on here, and I needed a stranger with unusual experience to find out what it was. This became known to the syndicate, you see, and the impersonation planned.

'Unfortunately for them, the plot to shoot you down into the sea failed. You proved more resourceful than they had foreseen. But perhaps you are beginning to appreciate that.'

Suddenly I remembered a brief scene of the inside of the plane and Jo trying to throw the wallet out of the window. I remembered snatching it back, and thought how lucky it was I had.

We came to the rock. It was still open. Gabriel took a small bomb from the pocket of his baggy suit, threw it into the hole, then uncoiled some very fine flex from it as we walked on again. 'That is for later,' he said.

We came in sight of the beach, but there was no sign of Muck still waiting.

'The reward for impersonating me to you being he could later go and collect my money at home?' I said.

'An added inducement,' Gabriel said. 'He ran a risk, but not of wearing make-up. He does look like you.'

'When I saw him in the hotel he was straw-blond and heavy black brows — '

'Make-up then, when it wasn't dangerous. For the dangerous part he had no need. He was a very good actor,' Gabriel said, almost reminiscently.

'In dealing with spies,' he went on, 'one

241

has to employ spies and the devices of spies. Actors can be inclined to overdo it. They are likely to be flamboyant where a spy should be just quiet and grey and natural.'

'But Muck had been here before?'

'Never. I have used him for certain crude work on Main Island. He has never been here until tonight.'

'You didn't show any surprise when you saw him, or her.'

'There's never any point in showing surprise. To keep it hidden, to accept what is meant to be a surprise very often confuses the enemy. Muck had meant to land as you. In the event he had to be a woman — someone I and some of my men would know. What he intended to do in the way of explanation I don't know.

'By the time it would be required, he hoped, the necessity for it would have gone,' he said calmly.

On the hillside across the beach I saw the grey Land-Rover crawling up the winding road, appearing now and again between the trees.

'How many are there?' I said, pointing.

He smiled.

'It's an optical illusion. There are two, but only one shows at a time. I like to keep a surprise in reserve.'

'You are still sure that Lee was the spy,' I said. 'But it seems to me the spy must be the one who switched the camera lines. That would suggest an engineer rather than a headphone man.'

'Addison, you think, or Heinz?'

'I've never seen either. It's up to you. But from what you say it's too late to matter.'

'I cannot tell that unless we have the microfilm.'

'Oh! the details are there, are they?'

'Details of the invasion, yes.'

'Are you so sure about Jim's loyalty?'

'One should never be sure of loyalty or women. I think he would try to be faithful, even against his better judgement.'

'Where is he now?'

'He is looking after Muck. If Muck is dead, Jim is loyal. If he is alive, that would be a pity. What I am more concerned about is the beach. If we had the microfilm, we would know.'

'Okay then,' I said. 'I'll unload.'

My hips were heavy with the two pistols, and I saw Gabriel's look of amusement as I unloaded the arsenal and felt in my pockets for my penknife.

'Here, hold these,' I said, giving him the guns.

I searched again, each pocket, but I well remember I had the knife in my left pocket, the pocket, where, at that time I'd shifted out Lee's gun. The pocket where I would have had nothing but the knife.

And then I remembered Lee lying there, staring up at thc moon with his mouth open.

I ran back up the path to the rock and the corpse. I knew he had a knife in his back, because I'd seen it jutting when he'd come out head first and before he'd rolled over.

As I turned him on his side, I knew before the knife came into view that it was going to be mine.

And there it was, open and stuck into his back up to the hilt. The microfilm had gone.

It could have been that I had dropped the knife, and someone had picked it up. But the unluck of that was too much to swallow.

More likely I had been seen hiding the film in the knife, and that the watcher had picked my pocket. Lee could have seen through the keyhole, perhaps.

That meant Gabriel had been right about him.

But who had killed him? Who had taken the knife perhaps knowing what was in it? Who had tried to destroy the film before?

Jo.

10

Some things are so obvious when at last you see them that you can't see how you didn't spot them before. Jo was one of those. From the start I had had no evidence that her husband had been after me, only that Jo had said. She had started our flight from the hotel.

She had been somewhere round the back of the flight hut signalling to the cruising Anglia belonging to the millionaire, Harz. By that means Harz would know how we were going, and where, and the Piper at Flamingo Bay had thus been alerted.

The idea being, simply to get rid of me so that Muck could take my place on Shark Island. After that he could sail away and grab my small fortune.

Sail away from what?

I left Simpson/Lee and went back to where Gabriel stood watching the shore. It was near dawn then.

'It's gone,' I said. 'Some bastard stole my knife.'

'Pity, but I think it is too late,' he said. 'It is an hour to dawn. The attack will start then.'

'The attack?'

'They hope to grab my island. It would put them in a position to control all this part of the world. There would be no secrets from them. They wouldn't play it as I do, as a salesman. They have the money they want. All that remains for them is power.'

'Who? The millionaire syndicate?'

'Who else? You were to be the Trojan Horse — or rather your effigy, in the name of Muck. Now unfortunately, Muck is in a dilemma. He has failed them. He has failed me. It is a moment for his sincere regrets.'

A voice began to crackle from his pocket.

'Come in,' he said, bringing a small radio from his pocket.

'Four boats plotted heading this way, bearing eight-five, eight miles, thirty knots.'

'Anything behind or near?' Gabriel asked.

'Nothing at all. Nothing flying, either.'

'Out,' said Gabriel and pushed the set back in his pocket. 'Observe the situation, Jonathan. They have four cruisers, each having say, ten, fifteen armed men. Sixty. My ordinary workers have been bought. They will follow whichever side wins. You get the drift?'

'How many men in your patrols?'

'Four in each Land-Rover. The operators will defend the radio rooms. They will be the last to give in.'

'The patrols are armed with what?'

'Automatic rifles, grenades, tear gas bombs. The usual. I have never really done more than toyed with such a situation as this. If I hadn't, we could have mined the beach.'

He shrugged.

'There is a faint hope,' I said. 'That is, if the plane still flies.'

'It will,' he said, watching me slit-eyed. 'I told Jim to make sure.'

'I see one patrol truck over there on the cliff road. Where's the other? It could take us down to the plane. Thirty knots. Eight miles. Say it gives us a quarter of an hour.'

'Sure.' He spoke into his radio. 'Send number two on to east drive now.'

He began to walk further down the path, and I followed him. He seemed unrattled. Whatever may be said of his activities, getting into a flap wasn't one of them. It's good to have a man to stand beside who takes it all as a matter to be dealt with, and not to be shocked by.

The Land-Rover came down the curling road within a minute. It stopped by us. We clambered in beside the driver. The other three men were in the back part. The truck went on down and soon we were spraying the soft dry sand of the high part of the beach.

The plane was there under the cliff, pinned down. As soon as we got by it, the men in the back jumped out, unlashed the anchor lines and took up the screw pickets from the firmer ground where she stood. The driver acted foreman. It was clear they had done this many times before, probably for Mel. Gabriel stood by me.

'And then?' he said.

'Get yourself an auto rifle, some grenades, perhaps a gas bomb or two.'

He chuckled softly.

'Jonathan, they have four fast cruisers, full of men and all armed.'

'Okay, so they do. You have eight men, armed and mobile. But at thirty knots the boats can switch from this beach round to your little harbour and be ashore before the patrols can meet them.'

'They won't try to land on the hard,' he said. 'The only way up from there is by lift in the cliff. Easily mastered by my operators.'

'So this and the beach next door are the most likely?'

'They could try others, but they might well expect to overcome resistance. One big blow here could defeat our patrols. The rest of my people have been paid not to fight, as I told you.'

We both turned and looked towards the plane. They had started the engine.

We had ten minutes from then.

Gabriel got some of the arms he wanted from the Land-Rover and we went on to the aircraft, he bulging with grenades. He shouted to one of the men to bring more, and gas bombs. I didn't take a rifle, though there were a couple of spares. My pistols were enough to give confidence.

If any such commodity would be needed in less than ten minutes from now.

It was an odd feeling to be facing an actual battle in a place where there was no law to stop it. There would be no retribution here. Just a winner and a loser.

Gabriel stowed his armaments by the right seat and thoughtfully bashed the sliding window right out with the butt of his rifle. That would let him lean well out with his gun.

No wonder he had kept his own for so long. He was cool and thought well of details.

The engine seemed to be running normally. As I got in the pilot's seat I saw the fuel was well down. We had used a lot in skirmishing over Flamingo Bay and then fighting the winds.

It was dead calm and hot on the beach then. The moon was low on the western sea, and although it was still only a short time from dawn, no streak of light showed in the eastern sky.

I just thought of it as another West Indian instant dawn. Funnily, I didn't think of Gertie. There were, I suppose, too many other things to think about.

During this time the radio kept coming in with bearings, distance and speed of the invasion boats. The boats were holding a steady course, as if they weren't frightened of anything.

We got in and I ran up the engine. She was all right.

There was no wind. I taxied round until we got on to the firm sand and then stopped, nose heading the longest way of the beach, that was south-east.

The radio kept chanting out the position of the boats while we sat behind the spluttering motor. We kept our eyes to the eastern horizon, but saw nothing of the invaders.

'Why don't we go?' Gabriel said.

'I reckon the nearer the island they get, the less room they'll have for manoeuvre. If we catch them in between the horns of the bay it'll give us more chance than out in the open sea.'

'Okay. You're captain,' he said. He flipped the catch of his rifle up and down. It was the only sign he gave of tension.

With six minutes to go I made out white bursts far out on the black sea. The yellow light of the moon was dying in the west. There was no glow at all from the east.

At four minutes the white smears were clear, arrowing towards the beach.

I opened the throttle. We started off across the beach, the controls heavy in the still air. Then the heaviness went, she came alive and we unstuck after only a short run. So the first of my nightmares had been beaten.

I made a climbing turn right, easing the throttle back to climbing revs somewhere over the top of the cliff. I didn't want to be silhouetted against the sky.

We came low over the house and its

outbuildings. It looked like a white fort amid the palms and colour bursts of flower bushes. Turning still, we came round full circle and saw the white arrows in the sea heading towards the horns of the beach. They looked as if they were running into the jaws of a giant stag beetle.

I cut speed to the lowest, trying to hover in slow curves over the top of the island. Now and again we could see down to the beach. The Land-Rover had withdrawn behind a fringe of trees on the beach, waiting in ambush.

The second one was still on the cliff road, just visible under the fingers of the trees.

The white arrows were sharp on the black sea, almost between the horns of the bay. I turned away, keeping low over the topmost trees of the island.

We made a full turn and then I opened up and held the nose down. She gained speed quickly. The treetops tore by underneath, snatching at the wheels. Gabriel clicked the catch of his gun like a cricket rubbing its legs together. The sound of the wind was hard and noisy in his wide-open window.

We came over the top of the cliff. The bow waves of the invasion boats were dead ahead and appeared to be within the horns of the bay.

We tore down the slope towards the beach, levelled a little and then sped out, fifty feet over the water. The boats were swelling now, faster and faster.

I went down almost to touch the smooth sea and we went directly at the bows of number two boat from the left. He started to swerve. I held on to him, ruddering very slightly, plenty of throttle on.

I held it till it seemed we were going to ram, and then I opened wide, hopped up and banked slightly, just clearing his short mast as he sheered off in a wild turn.

I pulled her round in a steep turn and in the middle of it looked up through the roof, which gave me a long view across the sterns of the boats — or three of them.

The one I had headed off hit number one on the left. What kind of a crash there was I don't know, but the boats seemed to be stuck together in a great burst of water, and men were somehow flying about in the spray.

'Great God!' Gabriel said, then put his gun out of the window as we levelled and went back.

I headed over the sinking boats, and he fired down at men struggling in the boiling white waters by their broken, drifting craft. The boats were still jammed, one into the side of the other, and a lot of wreckage floated in the troubled sea.

I steep turned again. The remaining two boats had split up, one running for the eastern horn of the bay, the other going diagonally for the beach. I chased that one.

As we came up off the sea over his mast, Gabriel chucked down a lapful of grenades. He hit with one, but it was somewhere at the stern and we got hit by several rifle bullets.

That one was not going to be put off, for he didn't turn at all from his onset on the beach.

I had turned over and past him so we went for the boat now heading for the open sea. He swelled up ahead of us. I kept about fifty feet up and Gabriel got ready at his window.

My blood froze when he pulled the pins out of three grenades and just held them, judging our speed to the second.

The first one fell astern but went off in the air and I saw riflemen duck and fall back into the well of the cruiser. The second one burst in the water, way out.

We were beginning to bucket and jump. The wind was coming in again.

The third grenade burst ahead of the boat. We went on, and steep turned back on it again. We hadn't been hit at all that time, I think.

'If you can steady over her I'll hit!' he said, pulling more pins.

'We'll have to come round the back again,' I said.

We ripped by her, going the opposite way. Gabriel tossed out a bomb, just as a reminder, for he couldn't have hit her.

But I did see men on her decks ducking or lying flat.

Which meant that as far as a fight between air and sea was concerned they had conceded victory.

Go back on them, go back!' he said.

'They've chucked in,' I said. 'They just want to go home.'

'Go back,' he said. 'I want to try.'

So I did. I got her up astern of the boat and then throttled her back, pulled the nose up and got her down to fifty. So at twenty knots difference, we sailed over the port side of the motor cruiser.

We got shot. We got a lot of shots, through the wings and in the cabin. I held her steady and then Gabriel tossed two bombs down.

I thought he had missed. Nothing happened as I opened up and banked into a turn. Then through the roof I saw the boat swell as if somebody pumped it up. A bright red flash shot up out of the well, rising high into the dawn. Smoke followed the tongue of fire and then the whole pillar was swept and torn aside.

At the same instant we seemed to be shoved bodily sideways across our track. I steadied up, but she was bucketing and tearing like a mad horse.

The instruments started dancing about. Strips of fabric, tears started by bullet holes, began to strip off the wings. The shrieking of wind sounded even above the battling engine.

Gertie was back.

Even in the bay the sea was whipped up and turned into white shreds with the fury of the returning storm. Holding her nose roughly towards the beach I saw the long strand of sand passing sideways in jerks across our front, and the whole machine half stalling in the gusts.

'We've had this, G!' I shouted.

'Land!' he bellowed. 'You did before!'

The gust fell suddenly. So did we. We recovered with full engine just off the sea. Spray hit the screen and streamed off it.

It was just one bounce towards the end. We tore and jerked in the air over the wrecks of the two boats, and the scattered men now fighting the white bursts of the wild sea streaming towards the beach.

'We're going to crash,' I shouted at him. 'Toss out the bombs. Get rid of them!'

He did, thoughtfully pulling the pins out as he braced himself against the wild bumping of the aircraft.

We were close in to the beach then. One gust turned us right over on to our side, and I could feel that another such would pull the wings off.

The only hope was to motor into the sea, as near into wind as I could guess, and to wish that the wind would hold just long enough to let us down.

It didn't. Just when it seemed we might it just whistled up and took us right over on to our back a few feet over the water. There was no question of doing anything. Just of letting the seat belts hold and to wonder what we would wake up in.

It was just surf we hit. There was a lot of it, crashing against the cabin and tearing the wings. We were being thrown about on the sand by the undertow, dragged round, shoved and pushed like some toy.

He shouted something, and then I was glad for his wide open window. We both got out of that. Outside we got thrown against the fuselage by the sea repeatedly and in the end I almost gave in from pain and exhaustion.

But when the rudder and tailplane was swung round away from me in a burst of sea, I saw Gabriel ahead, crawling up the beach, his suit stuck to him except at the edges where it streamed like tatters in the wind.

I fought off everything, tow, undertow, wind, rain and my wish to die. Slowly, I got on to the beach until a mighty breaker took me right in the backside. I was smothered, almost drowned, tossed, tumbled and thrown right up the beach.

Suddenly I found myself out of the sea, fingers dug in the sand just being torn apart by wind and hailing rain. That was easy by comparison. I began to feel better and scurried on all fours like a crab, away from the reach of the sea.

* * *

They found Harz washed up amongst a lot of other bodies. The last boat which had made for the beach had turned to run and had been caught by the storm.

261

They say it lasted quite a few minutes and then turned upside down, and they didn't see it any more.

They found a lot of Muck. He had tipped off the bomb Gabriel had left in the hidey hole in Simpson's rock.

The funny part was, they didn't find Jo.

Three days after that, when Gertie had finally whirled itself out in the Atlantic, Mel came over in a new aircraft got from the insurance.

He came to fly me to the nearest port where I could get a plane home. It was a nice aircraft, twin engined, four seats and with a lot of luggage space behind them in a locker.

We took off along the beach. He juggled with the trimmer.

'I don't get the trim of this thing,' he said. 'She feels tail heavy.'

'Perhaps you have a sting in the tail,' I said, as we unstuck.

We had.

When we landed at the airport we found Jo was in the locker.

My feelings, when she came tumbling out, crumpled, dirty-faced and with her hair all over the place, were mixed as a plum pudding. We had landed then, and rolled to a stop in a park. A couple of attendants came running, but Mel switched off and made a washout sign with his hands. The runners nodded, grinned and turned away to other work.

'Well, well,' Mel said, dryly. 'You certainly take your baggage with you, sport.'

She leant on the back of my seat and looked at me in a way that gets in and wriggles about inside me.

'Missed me?' she said.

The close-grained impudence of it!

'Missed you?' I said. 'Why, the whole ruddy island's been searching three days for you!'

'I wouldn't have been so hard to find if Gabriel hadn't put a bomb in that stone. I got sealed down there with nothing but water pouring down the wall and six cases of baked beans.'

'That's a lie, to start with. The bomb was cleared after the armada was dissipated. Incidentally, Harz was there. Drowned, I'm afraid.'

'Yes, I know,' she said.

'Oh, you knew that?'

'I saw him on the beach.'

'If you saw his body on the beach you weren't shut in the hidey hole, because the corpses were cleared by noon that day, after the storm went.'

'Well, I heard about it, then. But you see, it means the end of the Syndicate. Harz's dead and the other three will shrink when they know Gabriel is looking for them. Some things money doesn't buy. One of them is Gabriel's goodwill.'

'He very near lost that island,' Mel said. 'If those boats had got there, he wouldn't have stood a chance. There's a lot of luck in these things.'

'By the way, Jo,' I said, 'did you kill Lee, by any chance?'

'Good gracious! Me?' She looked horrified.

She could look anything on tap, I thought. And yet, damn my idiot instincts, if that didn't make her more attractive. The sheer ability to put it on, take it off, laugh, cry, sparkle and dim made her all the more exciting.

I don't know what my expression was

as I watched her, but Mel said sharply: 'Watch what you're doing sport!'

Too late. It was starting all over again. I hauled myself back by the scruff of my mental neck.

'There was a roll of film in the knife,' I said.

'Was there?' she said.

'It showed all the defences of the island and how to slosh them down. Information worth considerable pennies.'

'You know what I'd like?' she said, looking intently and mischievously into my eyes. 'I'd like a bath and a drink and a ticket to London.'

'Why don't you drown yourself, Johnny?' Mel said. 'You'll get to the same place quicker.'

She ignored him and kept smiling at me.

She knew I couldn't resist it. I didn't want to. After all, Gabriel was safe now, and whatever she had done to cheat him was over. She couldn't do anything to me. That is, I didn't think so.

THE MAYHEM MADCHEN
THE DEATH IMPORTER
THE THUG EXECUTIVE
A WREATH OF BONES
THE CASE OF THE FEAR MAKERS
A FALL-OUT OF THIEVES
THE FARM VILLAINS
FATE OF THE LYING JADE
THE LIGHT BENDERS

*Other titles in the
Linford Mystery Library:*

THE GIRL HUNTERS

Sydney J. Bounds

Doll Winters was a naïve teenager, who fantasised about being a film character. But when Gerald Dodd committed a brutal killing, she found herself starring in a real-life murder drama — as the star witness! And when Dodd tries to silence her, Doll turns for help to the famous private detective Simon Brand. Then a further terrifying attempt on her life forces her to go on the run. But can Brand find her before the killer can?

CRIME MOST FOUL

George Douglas

When a teenager attacks an old
lady, her best friend, Detective
Constable Sheldon, wants revenge.
Chief Superintendent Bill Hallam of
North Central Regional C.I.D. forbids
Brenda Sheldon to get involved in
the case. Ignoring the ban her
investigation, aided by Dave Morgan,
leads her to a drug racket in Deniston.
The trail is obscure until Molly Bilton
tries to help a man involved with the
drug pushers, but finds the man
murdered, and her own life in danger.

THE GILDED KISS

Douglas Enefer

It was the key to a most baffling exploit for Dale Shand, but a lot was to happen to him and the bewitching Linda Travers before he found it. For her, Shand leaves his new headquarters in Baker Street, London, to travel across Europe and back, where he follows a trail of murder and big-time art theft. In a high-octane adventure, he encounters a sinister Spaniard, a mysterious girl and a missing heir — all enmeshed in the tangled web.

BIGFOOT

Richard Hoyt

Private Detective John Denson and his partner, Willie Prettybird, are helping Russian scientist, Dr. Sonja Popoleyev, in her search for the legendary Bigfoot. And with big money at stake, they also have competition in thcir quest, including Alford and Elford Pollard, local bigfoot hunters. But Elford is murdered before the expedition has begun. Soon, the searchers scramble for traces of the creature. But the murderer isn't finished yet, and Denson and his party are on the endangered species list.

WHOO?

Richard Hoyt

When John Denson undertakes to clear a Washington State client of a marijuana charge, he finds himself in spotted owl country. He discovers that the tiny bird is up against the logging industry. A spotted owl is found murdered, and Denson's partner, Willie Prettybird, wants him to investigate. But then Jenny MacIvar of the Fish and Wildlife Service is murdered; a simple marijuana case turns into a hunt for a killer, and Denson may be the next victim.

GUNMAN AT LARGE

George Douglas

In the height of its summer season Whitsea is suffering from an outbreak of robberies; Chief Inspector 'Jack' Spratt wonders whether more than one gang is involved. Sergeant Dick Garrett gets into the act when a gunman cuts loose on a caravan site, and when masked men hold up the Palladium box office. A snout, who tries to play both sides against the middle, makes complications which are heightened by a murder before Spratt can clear the Whitsea files.